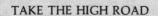

TAKE THE HIGH ROAD

TAKE THE HIGH ROAD

Mist on the Moorland
by
Michael Elder

This book is published by
SCOTTISH TELEVISION
Cowcaddens
Glasgow G2 3PR

in conjunction with
MAINSTREAM PUBLISHING
7 Albany Street
Edinburgh EH1 3UG

ISBN 0 906391 89 X

Typeset by Studioscope in conjunction with
Mainstream Publishing.
Printed in Great Britain by Collins, Glasgow.

To
Derek, Eileen, Ken, Robin, Judith, Paul, Lesley,
Bob, Gwyneth, Jay, Caroline, Joan, Iain, Marjorie, Alec,
John, Muriel, John, Jimmy and Jeannie
For being in it

Executive Producer ROBERT LOVE
Producer   BRIAN MAHONEY
Script Writers   PETER MAY
                    TOM WRIGHT
                    BILL CRAIG
                    WILLIAM ANDREW
                    MICHAEL ELDER
                    SUE GLOVER
                    JANICE HALLY
Series Devised by   DON HOUGHTON

Chapter One

1

Davie Sneddon slammed the receiver back in the cradle and sat glowering at it, biting the nail of his left forefinger. Who the hell did she think she was, ringing up like that without the slightest warning and issuing orders as if she owned him?

Last time she had been here she was putty in his hands. Well, almost. But she'd been on her own then, a poor forlorn little figure who might have aroused pity if she hadn't aroused contempt. There had been times when she'd flushed angrily at his taunts and insults and it had brought a liveliness to her face which was normally lacking.

Now, of couse, he'd have to be careful, and he knew he was not looking forward to the change.

This time she would have her husband with her.

Why had no one warned him? Was it simply that now that she was back with her husband she was going to extract some kind of revenge—a plot on her part to wrongfoot him? Or was it that they didn't think it worthwhile warning him, that he was only a hired servant anyway, and would do what his lords and masters ordered?

He swung up from the desk in his office and stared gloomily out of the window.

It was high summer and the leaves on the trees round Letir-Falloch drooped listlessly in the midday heat. Beyond, the loch looked like polished brass.

Dammit, it was a bit much. And the housekeeper was on her annual fortnight's holiday. Had they known that, and had they deliberately picked their time and were they giggling at the thought of him running around like a knotless thread trying to find sheets and pillow cases and wondering which tin to open for lunch?

He turned back to the telephone and, picking up the receiver, dialled a London number.

"Give me Mr Davenport, please," he said to the female voice which answered him.

"Mr Davenport is engaged at the moment," said the voice with professional briskness. "Can I take a message?"

"I want Mr Davenport in person and I want him fast. Tell him it's David Sneddon from Letir-Falloch," he said.

"One moment, please," said the voice, the professional briskness undaunted, and the line went dead.

He held on, staring sightlessly out of the window until the brisk female voice suddenly said, "Go ahead, please," and the rich voice of Charlie Davenport broke in on his thoughts.

"Sneddon? How you doing, boy?" he said.

"Listen," said Sneddon. "What's all this about the Shaws coming here today? Both of them."

"That's right. They are."

"No one told me."

"Someone must of or you wouldn't of known."

"Mrs Shaw rang from Auchtarne to say that they're getting the next ferry. Not much warning, is it? And the housekeeper's on holiday . . ."

"Stop flapping, Sneddon. They don't want nothing. A quiet fortnight on their own. What you might call convalescence for Harry. Just what the doctor ordered. You make sure he gets a good break, know what I mean? I want him back in London undamaged a week Wednesday. All right? That's my boy."

The receiver went dead and Sneddon was left holding it, rage beginning to tremble in him.

The indignity of it! Acting as nursemaid, fetching and carrying, making beds, washing dishes! He could, of course, get someone from Glendarroch to come and help him with the chores. But he wasn't going to make himself beholden to any of *them*. The Shaws would just have to take what he felt inclined to do himself and make the best of it.

He glanced at his watch. They'd be at the Glendarroch jetty in half an hour if the ferry was on time.

He muttered a curse under his breath and left the office, crossed the kitchen to the back door, his footsteps echoing on the stone flags, and headed for the garage where Mrs Shaw's car had lain since she had left it on her departure for America.

If he were going to have to fetch and carry for the
Shaws as well as conduct the business of Letir-Falloch at
least he'd make sure that he used as much of the Shaws'
own property as he could.

2

The summer weather had brought a steady trickle of
tourists into the shop, and though the purchases had
generally been small—sweets for the children and
suntan lotion—Isabel had cause to feel pretty happy
with the turnover when Brian came back for lunch after
his morning round of peat deliveries.

She was about to turn the notice at the door to
"Closed" and lock up when yet another stranger
appeared and she opened the door to let him in.

"Why, thank you, ma'am, you're very kind," he said.

His voice was low and rich and American and he
himself looked elderly. He was very tall and thin and his
sparse hair was grey at the temples and almost non-
existent on top. His shoulders were bowed as though
through years of stooping rather than from trying to get
through low doorways, for he was not as tall as that.

His clothes belied his accent. They were the sort of
things the gentry wore on casual occasions. There was
an old Harris tweed jacket with leather elbow and cuff
patches which must have been very hot in this weather,
an old pair of grey trousers and an open-necked white
shirt with green checks which exposed his wiry neck. In
his hand he held a crumpled soft hat which might in its
youth have been white.

He stood blinking in the gloom of the shop after the
brilliance of the sunshine outside.

"Can I help you?" Isabel asked.

"I'm seeking directions, ma'am," he said. "To Letir-
Falloch."

"Oh, yes," said Isabel. "Have you a car?"

"I hired one this morning in Auchtarne. They told me
it was only about twelve miles."

"Yes, so it would still be a fair walk from Glendarroch.
You go straight on along the road and it's on the right

hand side. The drive with the iron gates about five miles from here."

"I'm most obliged to you," said the stranger and he made her a little bow which was as endearing as it was old-fashioned.

She and Brian watched him go and then she locked the door.

"A nice man," she said, taking off her apron and laying it behind the counter.

"Yes, if it wasn't for the accent you'd hardly know he was an American," said Brian dryly.

"I wonder what he wants at Letir-Falloch?" Isabel mused as she led the way through the back shop towards the living room.

"He's probably casing the joint."

"What?"

"Casing the joint. It's what they do in gangster pictures when they're plotting the way into the bank."

She headed for the cooker in the kitchen.

"No, but there's only Sneddon there at the moment. I wouldn't have thought a man like that and a man like Sneddon would have much in common."

"Very little. Since you didn't ask him yourself you'll just have to wait till Mrs Mack finds out and gives you all the gory details at second hand."

She flung a dish towel at him and Brian grinned and dropped into a chair. As she heated the soup she found herself humming under her breath. The realisation stopped her. It was a long time since she had last done that. Not since Jimmy had left. And not for quite a while before that, what with one thing and another. Maybe things were beginning to look up again at last.

3

The loch was on its best behaviour that day. It was glassy smooth and the wake of the ferry was the only thing which disturbed it, stretching and spreading out endlessly behind them towards Auchtarne. There was absolute silence apart from the steady putter of the engine which only seemed to make it more profound.

Even the passengers seemed awed into silence in sympathy.

Eddie sat at the wheel as the headland loomed to starboard and the jetty crept into view. There were quite a few people on the ferry, tourists for the most part. He could hear the clicking of their cameras behind him as they recorded the hills beyond the loch, and the occasional gasps of sheer pleasure at the views constantly opening up before them.

But the two people who intrigued him most sat at the back, saying very little, sitting close together and from the occasional glance he had managed to steal at them he was pretty sure their hands had not been unclasped since they had first sat down in the boat at the pier at Auchtarne. She wore a dark blue open-necked shirt with rolled-up sleeves and a pair of jeans which almost matched. He was much more colourful, as though he were not so concerned at keeping a low profile as she was. He wore a multi-coloured short-sleeved shirt and a pair of red trousers. They had a couple of heavy suitcases with them.

What had brought her back? he wondered. After what had happened last time she was here, he would never have thought she would show her face in Glendarroch again. Logically he told himself that what had happened couldn't have been entirely her fault. It was very easy to blame someone you didn't know very well and who wasn't there to defend herself, and he was quite sure that Jimmy Blair had been as much to blame as she was, but the fact remained that it was primarily because of her that Jimmy had had to leave the village, nearly breaking Marion Cochrane's heart, causing distress to his parents and pain to many other local people too.

She had seemed embarrassed as she stepped on to the ferry. They had been the first to arrive at the Auchtarne pier, obviously having come off the Glasgow train at the station.

"Good morning, Eddie," she had said as he worked at one of the mooring lines, and he had recognised the voice before he turned to look at her.

"Hallo, Sally," he had said, and heard the lack of welcome in his voice.

She had nodded as though that was no more than she had expected and had turned to help the man into the boat in what looked like a motherly fashion.

And Eddie had recognised him too, of course, even before she had said, "This is Harry. My husband," in a non-committal tone of voice and with an almost negative gesture towards him with one hand. This was the great Vincent, just back from the States where he had been mobbed and torn apart coast to coast by rabid fans until illness had forced the abandonment of the tour when it was only three-quarters through. This was the man Sally had gone back to because she thought he needed her more than Jimmy did.

Perhaps she would have said more, told him what they were doing here, but he doubted it. The silence between them had stretched uncomfortably and then other people had arrived as sailing time approached and the chance had gone.

It was difficult not to keep looking round at them, almost as though he found it hard to believe they were really there. Eddie should have known better than to let the pop star image affect his preconceptions. Harry Shaw had been an electrician, he knew, who had played the gigs in his spare time until chance had picked him out for the celebrity treatment. He seemed very much smaller than he had expected and there was a vulnerability about him which didn't accord with the pop star image. The long dark hair which he knew from the publicity photographs had gone, cut to an ordinary length, but it was the dark eyes with a look old before their time and the pale face which caught his attention. He looked as though he were recovering from a recent illness. Which of course he was. He couldn't have been more than twenty-four and he looked thirty.

Harry was gazing round him, eyes wrinkled against the glare of the sun off the water, drinking in the scenery as though it were nectar. He didn't appear to be saying anything, but his face spoke it all. To him, this was good.

He caught Sally's eye and smiled in embarrassment at being caught so. She gave him a flicker of a smile in return, shy, uncertain, almost apologetic.

Eddie turned back as the ferry moved towards the jetty and slid the engine gently into reverse.

In view of the situation, what on earth were they coming here for? he wondered again. The question was as intriguing as it was baffling.

4

The house was out of sight of the road, and he deliberately left the car at the gates and, ignoring the Private notice, began to walk up the drive which was fringed with giant and ancient elms, feeling excitement fluttering inside him. This was the way to savour it, on his own feet. Not cooped up in a metal box on wheels.

It was utterly silent save for the distant bleating of sheep. Even the birds seemed dulled by the midday heat. He should have brought sandwiches from Auchtarne or bought something to eat from the village shop when he had asked directions to Letir-Falloch, but he hadn't thought about it and in fact he wasn't really all that hungry.

He walked slowly, letting the feel of the place seep into him. It is better to travel hopefully than to arrive, he thought and realised just how true that was. He was deliberately delaying the climax, savouring it as long as possible.

It was shady on the drive, the branches of the trees bending over him to form a green tunnel. On either side an iron fence bounded the land and out there the sun was very strong.

Clumps of rhododendrons, their flowers long dead, hid the view ahead, but as the drive swept round them the house came into view for the first time.

It was massive and four-square, the windows smaller than normal, no doubt to keep out the worst of the winter weather, though winter weather was hard to imagine at the moment, and he stood and looked at it, trying to analyse his feelings.

It was as though a long journey had come to an end. Or perhaps it was like a gentle awakening from a dream. It was very difficult to put a shape to his thoughts, because imagination kept intruding and in imagination he heard the laughter of children . . . Saw parasols and maids serving afternoon tea on the lawn . . . Cars driving off in the pre-dawn chill of the fall and returning in the late afternoon, their occupants wet and stiff and content, shotguns broken on their arms . . . Saw roaring log fires and malt whisky in crystal glasses and leather arm-chairs . . .

A rook cawed in the eaves and brought him back to the loneliness of reality, and he shook himself.

He walked across the gravel forecourt to the massive nail-studded front door. It was closed, and he pulled the bell. Far away within the house he heard it clanging and echoing into silence again. He stood waiting, drinking in the peace and the quiet.

No one came.

He rang again, and again listened to the bell pealing into silence within. It was funny how you could tell by the tone of a bell whether a house was empty or occupied.

After a moment or two he stepped back and looked up at the long façade of the house. There was a window open at the top, so the house was not completely shut up. He began to walk round it, peering rather guiltily through the windows as though he were intruding. The rooms were furnished but shrouded in dust sheets until he came to the back of the house and saw through one window that the room beyond was furnished as an office. A typewriter stood open on the table. A few papers lay screwed up in the waste-paper basket under the desk which was crowded with other papers. He felt reassured. The place was quite clearly occupied. It just so happened that he had called at the wrong time when there was no one in.

He returned to the front of the house and stood there on the front step, letting imagination take control. He felt his back straighten as he stood there and surveyed the view in front of him. All this was Letir-Falloch land. And somewhere not very far away . . .

Slowly, as if drawn by a string, he began to move away from the front of the house, but his steps didn't take him back to the drive and down to the gate. He moved off in the other direction, towards the trees and the hills, because somewhere over there, he felt sure, was where his quest would end.

5

"The point is we should have a second outboard so that when this one needs a service it can go away and get done properly and we'd still have one to use in the lifeboat," said Archie.

"But we haven't got one," said Sheila.

"No," said Archie. "We haven't."

"And meantime every time the lifeboat gets called out Eddie's taking a bigger risk."

"Now, I don't think that's quite true," said Mr Murdoch. "Though it *is* true that we haven't the funds to maintain the lifeboat to the standards required by the Royal National Lifeboat Institution, but then we are not a part of the Royal National Lifeboat Institution."

"I know that," said Sheila, and she turned away, clenching her hands together in frustration. The trouble was there was no one to blame. You couldn't look at someone and say, "It's all your fault."

"Don't worry, Sheila. There's no danger," said Archie.

"How can you be sure? What happens next time there's a gale and Eddie has to go out in this thing? Suppose the engine cuts out in the middle of the loch and he's left helpless?"

"That's extremely unlikely," said Murdoch.

"But it's getting more likely every day, isn't it?" said Sheila.

She tried to check the hysterical note which had crept into her voice. That wasn't going to help. If only she wasn't so worried about Eddie. And the fact that she was so worried about him worried her all the more. Eddie was all she had left and if anything happened to him in the lifeboat . . . It really didn't bear thinking about.

She stood looking at the grey inflatable standing on its carriage, its ridiculous name, *The Maggie*, painted on its side, almost as if she hated it. That was wrong. She shouldn't hate it. There had been deaths on the loch before the lifeboat came. Far too many deaths. There had been none since it arrived. It would be stupid to assume that there would be no more because of the lifeboat, but they had bought the thing and the men of Glendarroch manned it and lives had been saved and they all did their best to maintain it so that it was always ready for another errand of mercy, but there were times when it seemed like an enormous millstone round their necks.

"Look, Sheila, if it ever gets to the stage where we feel it's too dangerous to send the lifeboat out, then we won't send it out," said Archie.

"An attitude which would be of little help to those we were unable to save," said Mr Murdoch.

"Och, I know," said Sheila. "I know you're doing your best, Archie. It's just that . . . I don't want anything to happen to Eddie."

Archie patted her on the shoulder. "Don't you worry about Eddie," he said. "Eddie's a born survivor. You should know that."

She nodded and left the lifeboathouse, blinking in the sunlight, though she was fairly certain it was not the sun which had forced her eyes to water. As she went she heard the mutter of voices begin inside the lifeboathouse again, sunk so low that she obviously wasn't meant to hear what they were saying, and that fact alone made her worry even more.

The ferry was approaching the jetty and it looked fairly full. She stuck her hands in the pockets of her jeans and waited, seeing Eddie's dark head at the wheel. She waved and saw his head jerk in acknowledgement, but he was too busy to make any other form of greeting. She heard the engine note change and the bow wave slackened as he began to manoeuvre her slowly in.

She heard a vehicle draw up outside the Aqua-sports office and she turned to glance casually at the arrival. Then she looked harder. The car was familiar, but she hadn't seen it for a good many months — a beige Fiat Panda with an orange line which had been seen around here quite a lot not long ago.

She stared at it in surprise and then turned away again when she saw who was in it.

Sneddon.

She heard the door of the car slam shut and then his footsteps approach. She glanced at him and he nodded a curt greeting, standing some distance away and saying nothing.

"We don't often see you here," she said, feeling that something needed to be said.

"And this is too often." His voice was surly. "I've got enough to do without running around acting as unpaid chauffeur."

And he walked rudely away from her. She stepped on to the jetty and took the mooring line which Eddie threw to her and made it fast. As she did so she noticed a face she knew amongst the passengers.

Sally Shaw.

The passengers trooped slowly off the ferry and made their way on to dry land, clutching plastic bags and maps and plastic raincoats because, they had been warned, it almost always rains in Scotland and this weather had taken them by surprise. Mothers called children. A couple of Japanese were already taking photographs of the Aqua-sports office.

"Hi," she said as she helped Sally ashore.

Sally nodded and smiled and turned to take the case from the man who was with her, and then help him off. Sheila felt her heart thump as she recognised him. It was Vincent. In person. Not on the television or a record, but real, live and standing in front of her. He smiled at her and she felt herself smiling vacantly back like some weeny-bopper still wet behind the ears.

She watched as they took a suitcase each and Sally took his free arm and led him towards Sneddon who shook hands perfunctorily and unsmilingly and then led them towards the car.

"Stop simpering. He's booked, and I'm not," said Eddie as he jumped ashore and put an arm round her shoulders.

"Oh, yes, you are," she said, and she kissed him.

He began to make the mooring lines doubly secure.

"Good trip?" she asked.

"All right. Plenty of people. Funny what the sun brings out."

"What are *they* back for?" she asked as the car started and Sneddon turned it and headed towards the road with the Shaws sitting in the back.

"I don't know, but he's not well. Probably here for a rest. It must be his idea to come to Letir-Falloch. I don't think she'd come back after what happened with Jimmy."

"I wonder if he knows about that."

"I'm not going to tell him."

"Neither am I. But I bet Mrs Mack will if she ever gets the chance."

He straightened up.

"Any lunch," he asked.

"In the office."

6

Mrs Mack unlocked the door of the hall and stepped inside, forgetting for once to sniff at the state the Brownies had left it in that morning. The thought had crossed her mind that she would have to have a word with Brown Owl about it but this morning there were more important things to think of. She dumped her parcels on the table and went to the sink to prepare her cleaning material for a fresh attack on her surroundings. After a moment she stopped and looked discontentedly at her bucket and cloths. There was, she thought, little satisfaction to be gained by telling *them* her news. It was just a pity there was no one there to share it with her. Perhaps, she thought, it would be better to postpone the cleaning of the hall and go round to the village shop where there was sure to be someone who would listen to what she had to say, even if it were only Isabel.

The door opened and Mr Murdoch came in. Mrs Mack regarded him much as if he were an angel sent from heaven.

"Mrs Mack," he acknowledged. "A fine morning."

"Is it indeed," she said. "That I am not so sure of, Mr Murdoch. Not at all sure."

"Really?"

"Do you know what I saw on my way to the hall?"

"Not until you tell me, no."

"I saw a car in the village street . . ."

"The village street is often full of cars at this time of
the year, Mrs Mack. It's the tourists."

"I saw a car with three people in it."

She looked at him as though she expected that to
change his views.

"Mmph?"

"Three people. One of whom happened to be the man
Sneddon. And . . ." she drew herself up ready for the
climax . . . "the other was that Mrs Shaw."

The effect was instantaneous and as much as she
could have desired. Mr Murdoch's jaw dropped and he
sat down at the table.

"No!" he said.

"Indeed yes," she contradicted him, sitting down
opposite him.

"Well, well. Mrs Shaw." Mr Murdoch rubbed his chin
reflectively. "Now I wonder what she is doing back in
Glendarroch?"

"Indeed you may well ask, Mr Murdoch," said Mrs
Mack with unaccustomed generosity. "After all the
trouble she caused when she was last here. Breaking up
homes, leading our young people astray, ruining
perfectly innocent relationships . . ."

"Innocent relationships?"

"Jimmy Blair and Marion Cochrane," Mrs Mack
explained, apparently forgetting how she had
condemned the pair of them for the immorality of their
relationship when it had been in existence.

"Oh, them."

"But that's not all."

"It isn't?"

"There was a Third Person in the car with them.
Another man." She made the announcement as though
it might have been a polar bear.

"Who was it?"

"I do not know, Mr Murdoch. Some gigolo she is
installing at Letir-Falloch, no doubt, to take the place of
Jimmy Blair."

"It might be her husband," Mr Murdoch suggested
rather prosaically.

Mrs Mack paused for thought and felt a flash of disappointment pass through her.

"That is possible, I suppose," she admitted grudgingly. "But personally I have my doubts. And in any case I shall make it my business to find out. You will have a cup of tea, Mr Murdoch."

It was an order rather than a question, and he agreed, knowing that she would spend the time while making and drinking it discussing the matter further, that the discussion would take the form of a monologue and that he would be required to do little more than agree with her speculations. He was quite used to that, and a cup of tea would be most acceptable.

7

He sat down on a mossy bank. It had been a long and fairly arduous exploration but that was not the reason for his breathlessness. It was excitement, he told himself. The hunch had been right and the trip had been worth making.

He looked at the hollow in the land in front of him. It was bare of trees and bushes, a small natural amphitheatre. He had come across several cleared spaces like this and each one added to his certainty that he was right, though he didn't think he had yet found the specific one he was looking for.

To the right the ground sloped downwards towards Letir-Falloch House about a quarter of a mile away and conveniently screened from here by trees and bushes. He would like to examine the area closer to the house but thought it wiser to wait until he had established contact with the owner. To the left the hills rose to the more distant height of Ben Darroch. Straight ahead the cup of land narrowed into a defile where a stream — or, he supposed, they'd call it a burn here — meandered down towards the loch.

The ground itself was humped and irregular, the very kind of layout he had hoped to find. Just below the surface there should be untold treasures. With any luck . . .

"What the hell do you think you're doing here?" demanded a voice behind him, startling him with its suddenness.

He jumped to his feet, feeling his heart pounding, and found himself facing a man of medium height, dark-haired and with a glowering, bitter face.

"Good afternoon," he said. "I guess you must be the owner of this property, sir."

"I am not, but I'm his man of business, and I'd like to know what you think you're doing on private land."

This might not be too easy. The man was clearly short-tempered, almost as though he were looking for a fight.

"I called at the house about an hour ago. There didn't seem to be anyone in. I didn't think you would mind if I took a look round the estate."

"Well, I do mind. I take it you can read?"

"Of course."

"There's a notice at the gate which says *Private Property*. Isn't there?"

"Indeed there is . . ."

"You ignored it."

"I intended to explain my presence to the owner had I been able to find him."

"You can explain it to me instead. That notice means that we don't exactly welcome visitors, just to make it crystal clear to you."

"In that case I must apologise for my intrusion, sir."

"Apologise all you like so long as you take yourself off right now."

"I wonder if I might have a word with the owner, though? I reckon I may have some news for him which he would certainly appreciate . . ."

"I doubt if there's any news you could give the owner which would interest him very much at all."

"It's unfortunate that you should take this attitude . . ."

"Isn't it just? Now are you going to go or am I going to have you thrown out?"

"That will not be necessary, sir, but I have to say that I find your manner offensive."

"Listen, Yank. You're on land that I'm responsible for.

Now, I'm not going to bring the law into this because in these parts we don't pay too much attention to the law. It's too far away. We do our own judging and our own punishing. Do I have to make it any clearer?"

He felt a slow anger begin to burn in him. Normally, he told himself, I am a very mild sort of person. Perhaps too mild, but this man is beginning to make me annoyed. That is clearly his purpose: his tone of voice, his use of the word "Yank" in a derogatory manner, is all part of the effort to force an aggressive confrontation. An interesting psychological study. Or it would be so long as one were not personally involved as, willy-nilly, he had become.

"If that is your attitude, sir, there is little I can do about it, and I shall, of course, remove myself from the effects of your not very typical Highland hospitality. I will wish you a good afternoon."

"And good afternoon to you too. If you don't mind I shall see you off the policies. Just to make sure you go."

The man followed him from the cup of land which he had been surveying, over the rough ground between it and the house, during which he kept his eyes open for what he was looking for, but he had little opportunity to confirm whether it was there or not, across the gravel forecourt at the front of the house and down the drive to the gates where his car stood. He got into the car and drove off without another word passing between them. When he glanced in his driving mirror just before he entered the first bend in the road he saw the man standing at the gates looking after him, his brows still drawn in a petulant frown. In a way he looked disappointed. Perhaps because he had not been able to start a fight. If that were the case there was cause for some satisfaction in an otherwise highly unsatisfactory meeting.

8

It was a beautiful day again and Harry woke late. He lay for a while watching the reflection of the sunlight through the curtains and listened to the cawing of the rooks in the neighbouring elms, and then after a while he rolled out of bed with an eagerness which he hadn't known for a very long time.

Sally was in the kitchen downstairs, her head bowed over the table, and he crept up behind her and put his arms round her, feeling the firmness of her waist and breathing the perfume of her hair. She grunted — in surprise, he hoped, and not for any other reason — and turned to him.

"I let you sleep," she said.

"I noticed," he said, glancing at the clock on the kitchen wall. It showed five minutes to ten.

"Ready for breakfast?" she asked, breaking away from him and bending over the cooker.

"Just some tea and toast. Otherwise I won't be ready for lunch," he said.

Fifteen minutes later he pushed his cup aside and stood up.

"Seen Sneddon this morning?" he asked.

She shook her head.

"Good," he said. "I had a funny feeling when I woke up."

"Oh?"

"Aye. I *thought* this might be a good day."

"In what way?"

"No Seddon."

She smiled fleetingly.

"He'll be out on the estate somewhere," she said.

He stood at the window and looked at the distant hills and the woodlands round the house, feeling a sense of wonder that so much of it belonged to him. Well, in a way, it belonged to Charlie Davenport, he supposed, but it was in Harry's name for tax purposes, a sly dodge dreamt up by Charlie and his accountant to avoid paying the Government too much of the fabulous amounts of money which he was earning at the moment. Or rather, had been earning . . .

"It's funny," he said.

"What is?"

"All this. It's ours. Like a fairytale, isn't it? You feel that at midnight it's going to turn into a pumpkin."

"It doesn't."

"No. You'll know, of course . . . Know what?"

"What?"

"I envy you, having been here already. I should have been here too."

"Yes, you should."

There it was again, that edge of bitterness in her voice. He'd never heard that until he'd decided to come up here for a couple of weeks and he didn't know what to do about it. He didn't want to ask her what it meant because she might say things he didn't want to hear. Like how he'd left her to go to America and have a great time, and he didn't want to be reminded of how stupid he'd been . . .

"I'm going out," he said suddenly.

"Want me to come with you?"

He turned to look at her and saw again that worried, uncertain expression in her face. That rather than the bitterness had been lurking around her ever since she arrived in America to bring him home, and today for the first time it raised a feeling of irritation in him, irritation born of guilt.

"I'll be fine," he said and hurried out of the house before she could utter a word of protest.

He didn't take the car. The morning was too good for being enclosed, and he walked across the fields down towards the shore of the loch, looking in wonder at all that surrounded him.

It had been right to come here. This was the place which would do him good. Anything less like what he had experienced over the last three months would be hard to imagine.

His mind went back, as it kept on doing these days, to those times. From this distance it seemed a huge and terrifying jumble in which no one single event stood out clearly from the mass of noise and activity which had surrounded him for so long. The constant travel, the dozens of similar hotel rooms, luxurious and impersonal, the appalling coloured lights which had dazzled him as they burnt into his brain, the television interviews, press conferences at which he was expected to be bright and entertaining and give a considered opinion on every subject from The Russian Menace to the possibility of extraterrestrial life, the parties, receptions, the futile publicity stunts, and above all the meaningless screams and wavings of the thousands of fans. Fans everywhere. In the auditoriums, on the streets, outside the hotel. The offers of everything from a personal lifeline to God to heroin to women. There were times when he had been tempted, a very few times when he had succumbed and even more times when he had simply wanted to throw up. It all seemed like a terribly bad dream, but here at Letir-Falloch it was beginning to seem as though that must be all it was: a dream.

His mind shied away from the night in Los Angeles when the noise and the heat and the strobes had finally eaten completely into his mind, when the noise had swelled and receded like a pair of labouring lungs and he had felt something snap as the concert reached its climax of noise and he had mechanically waved his guitar at them and staggered off the stage without doing an encore while they screamed for more and would possibly have invaded the stage and come and torn him to pieces in their disappointment, and he had found himself crouched in a corner by the exit door, his arms protectively clasped round himself, his head on his chest, returning to a foetal position while distant voices, more distant than the baying of the crowd, had asked him if he was all right, if he wanted a glass of water, hey, Harry's flipped his lid, man, whaddya know, and then there were confused memories of hands lifting him and carrying him to his dressing-room and other hands lifting him and carrying him to the ambulance and then the clean, sterile bed and the smell of antiseptic and after all the noise had gradually emptied itself out of his mind he had heard himself crying like a baby: "Sally, Sally, Sally!"

After that there had been an endless time of prying hands and professionally gentle voices telling him not to worry, everything was all right, and that she was coming, though he didn't believe them, they were just being professionally soothing, and so he kept on calling for her.

And then the inexpressible relief of swimming into wakefulness one day and seeing that familiar face in front of him, familiar and yet unfamiliar, a face with

strain on it which had never been there before, and he
had cursed himself for allowing that strain to be put
there. He had put his arms round her and drawn that
dear head down to him and then he had just lain there
weeping silently and healingly. She was his and he was
hers and her presence brought a sense of reality to the
artificiality which he had been enduring for so long, and
he had been a fool ever to have left her behind, and he
was humbly grateful to her for coming to him when he
had called . . .

He reached the shore and found himself standing at
the edge of the marina. It was not finished yet, he knew,
but it was his money which was being used to build it,
and he supposed that Charlie Davenport knew what he
was doing, because he certainly didn't himself. Nor, at
this moment, did he wish to.

He could hear the sound of engines puttering around
the jetties and masts rose over the adjacent buildings like
a forest.

For a while he stood looking out across the water,
seeing the mirror-like surface reflecting the
surrounding hills, hearing the gentle lap of the tiny
wavelets at his feet washing on the shingle, and
suddenly he felt a huge desire grow in him.

Well, this was all his. Why shouldn't he take advantage
of it?

He walked to the marina office at the head of the main
jetty and stopped at the window.

"Got a boat?" he asked.

"Yes, sir," said the man inside. "We have several
available. What kind would you like?"

He hadn't been recognised, and that was perhaps the
most important thing of all today. No one knew who he
was. He wasn't Vincent to these people, he wasn't even
the owner of Letir-Falloch. He didn't actually own all the
hiring boats and the jetty and the marina itself.
Anonymity suddenly became a very precious thing.

Eventually when he had finished explaining exactly
what he wanted and he had felt great pleasure in paying
in cash for what was his anyway and when the
formalities had been completed as if he were a total
stranger and he had signed the form with the name of

Bernard Grant, which was one he had used before in an attempt to avoid recognition, the man came out of the office and led the way down the jetty to the spot where the hire boats were moored and pointed out the one which he realised he had been right to book because it was small and simple-looking.

"You know how to handle her, sir?"

"I'll manage," said Harry with a new-found confidence.

"Better not go too far out, sir. The weather's not going to last."

Harry looked at the utterly clear sky and the windless water and smiled, but the man shook his head.

"I know. Looks good, but the forecast's bad for the next few hours."

Harry didn't believe it. Nothing could go wrong today. This was the start of his climb back to health and strength. And a few hours lying in an open boat in the middle of a loch with a fishing line tied to his big toe, and never catching a thing, would make up for those weeks of noise and bedlam which still haunted his dreams.

"You'll find the lifejacket on the counter, sir," the man said.

"Fine," said Harry, wondering where you kept a counter on a boat.

The man hesitated as though waiting for him to do something about it, but he simply untied the boat and pushed it away from the edge of the jetty, watching with satisfaction the gap between boat and shore widen. It was as though with this action he were finally leaving the nightmares behind.

He waited till the man turned with some reluctance to go back to the office where an importunate queue was beginning to build up, and then he hoisted the sail, working inexpertly, and felt the boat suddenly come to life as the air caught the sail and made the little boat heel slightly under him.

Five minutes later he was moving slowly away from the marina. It was fortunate there was so little wind, because he really had no idea what to do. And somehow today that didn't matter. He sat at the back end and twiddled the — tiller, wasn't it? — and the boat seemed to respond, and he glanced back and saw the man from the office watching him from the head of the jetty, looking a bit worried, so he let go of the rope which was attached to the sail for a minute to wave to him and then grabbed it clumsily as the sail flapped and began to fall away.

Very quietly the little boat drifted out into the loch.

Chapter Two

1

The card was a plain white one with simple black lettering. It gave the name as David MacAulay and an address in New York State.

"He didn't say what he wanted?" Fiona asked.

"Just help," said Lorna.

Fiona nodded and sat down behind the desk again.

"All right, Lorna, show him in," she said, and then stopped her as she put her hand on the door handle. "Just a minute. What's the coffee situation? Is the percolator working?"

"Archie repaired it yesterday, so probably not."

"Oh, dear. Well, give it a shot, would you? If he's an American we can't offer him instant. Let's try to impress him. You never know. Maybe he wants to buy the estate."

Lorna smiled and went out, returning a moment later to usher in a tall, grey-haired, stooping man with a thin face and a gangly body. He wore faded but well-cut clothes and carried a rather disreputable soft white hat in his hand.

"Miss Cunningham?" he said, taking her outstretched hand in a firm grip. "A great pleasure, ma'am."

"Please sit down, Mr MacAulay," she said, and indicated a chair on the other side of the desk.

He lowered himself into it, folding the long body neatly as he did so, and sat with elbows on the arms of the chair, hands clenched under his chin as he looked benignly across the desk at her.

"Lorna said you were seeking help," she said.

"That's precisely it, ma'am. I trust you may be able to give it to me, or at least give me an indication of where I might find it."

"I'll certainly do my best."

She looked at him enquiringly.

"Let me explain, ma'am, that I am an archaeologist, and I am interested in neolithic and bronze age remains, particularly in this neighbourhood at this moment in time."

"I'm told there are a great many remains round this area," she said.

"You never said a truer word, Miss Cunningham. It may have been lucky in getting less attention from property developers and highway builders than most other parts of the country, and so a great many sites have remained virtually untouched. And there is one particular site which I got wind of some years back."

"And where is that?"

"It is on Letir-Falloch."

"Ah . . . You know Letir-Falloch, Mr MacAulay?"

He hesitated in a curious way and then nodded.

"I have been there this very day, ma'am."

"And?"

"And I'm afraid I got shown the way out. Pretty smartly, too."

Fiona nodded.

"By a dark man with an Irish accent?"

"My knowledge of British dialects is not very reliable, ma'am, but my ear did tell me that the man was not local."

"Sneddon," she said feelingly.

"He did not offer me his name, so I can't confirm that, but he did say he was acting on behalf of the owner."

"That's Sneddon."

"Now, this is where I need help, ma'am. I was hoping to visit with the owner but this man was — unco-operative. I wondered if perhaps you might be able to put me in touch with him?"

Fiona shook her head regretfully.

"I'm afraid I can't, Mr MacAulay. The wife of the present owner left Letir-Falloch some time ago. We've seen and heard nothing of her since, and we have never clapped eyes on her husband at all."

"You've no idea where they might be so that I could communicate with them?"

Fiona shook her head.

"None at all. There may be people in the village who would know, but I doubt it."

She felt sympathy for him as she saw his face fall in

disappointment.

"Well, now, if that isn't the darnedest thing," he said. "I beg your pardon, Miss Cunningham. The man I met was almighty rude and I should have enjoyed the chance of going over his head."

"Not an easy thing to do with Sneddon," said Fiona.

"And I don't really fancy going back there and pleading with him. You have no influence with this man Sneddon?"

"None whatsoever, I'm afraid. I don't think anyone in the village has. There has been — friction between him and us from the day he arrived, and his presence here since then has done nothing to lessen it."

The door opened and Lorna appeared with a coffee tray. MacAulay got courteously to his feet as she came in. She put the coffee tray down on the desk and withdrew, and for a minute or two Fiona was engaged with the formalities of offering coffee and cream and sugar and hearing what an excellent cup it was. Thereafter the conversation lapsed into a thoughtful silence.

"I wish I could help you, but I really don't see how I can," she said. "Except with a word of advice. Sneddon's a dangerous man. He's not above taking the law into his own hands."

He nodded and she saw that there was a look of quiet determination on his face. This was a man who, she felt, would not crumple under Sneddon's bluster and threats, but she also felt a stirring of concern. He was elderly and could be frail and she wouldn't give much for his chances if Sneddon became physical.

"If you would ever care to look over Glendarroch land, Mr MacAulay, you would be more than welcome," she said.

He thanked her with great sincerity, but she could see that that was not the prime object of his visit. He had his eyes fixed in one specific direction. The conversation turned to the beauty of the district and as he extolled its merits she detected a deep yearning in him, a yearning which she had often detected in visiting Americans, especially those with Scottish names, but in this case it seemed deeper and more sincere than most.

What was it about this country, she wondered, which

held its wandering children in such a firm grip?

They conversed for some time on ordinary topics and she found him shrewd and humane and extremely likeable. As she warmed to him she began to wonder about his own ancestry. After all, MacAulay, although not at all an uncommon name, was one which was very clearly remembered in these parts, but she left her enquiries too late. He refused the offer of a second cup of coffee, rose and put his empty cup on the tray.

"I shall not take up any more of your valuable time, Miss Cunningham," he said. "Thank you for your courtesy."

"I'm just sorry not to be able to offer you any more practical help," said Fiona.

She accompanied him to the door and into the reception room where Lorna sat at her typewriter. Mr MacAulay stopped in front of her.

"You have a magical hand with coffee, ma'am," he said. "It was very much appreciated."

Lorna smiled in pleasure and surprise and he followed Fiona out into the huge stone-flagged hall and across to the front door. As Fiona opened it a gust of wind suddenly blew in, making her hold on to the door a little more firmly than she had been prepared to do. And at the same time the sun suddenly disappeared behind a cloud, leaving the view outside grey and dull.

"They forecast a break in the good weather later today," said Fiona, "but only for a short time."

"The one thing I dislike is rain," said Mr MacAulay. "It makes digging so heavy."

They shook hands and she watched as he climbed into his car and drove away down the drive, feeling pleased that from his final remarks he had obviously not given up the idea of pursuing his quest on Letir-Falloch.

2

Harry awoke shivering and for a moment wasn't sure where he was. He felt panic well up in him at the unfamiliar surroundings. There was a crick in his neck and he was aching in every bone from the unnatural position in which he had fallen asleep.

The boat, of course. That was it. Somehow he'd made his way out to the middle of the loch, the boat drifting rather than sailing, and then he had thrown out the anchor at the front, untied the rope holding up the sail and lowered it so that the boat would stop and he had lain idling there, not moving, suspended in total silence and immobility. Around him the hills had risen from the shore of the loch, green and brown and craggy on their heights above the tree line, slightly hazy in the brilliant sunlight, while the fields below had been picked out in patchwork colours of green and yellow and brown and russet as the corn ripened and the cattle and sheep cropped the grass.

He had sat there, not thinking, just drinking it in. He came from the town, of course. Born and brought up in Glasgow, and until recently the thought of living in the country had filled him with horror. Empty, lonely, no buses, no trains, no people, no nothing, but after the American experience when there had been too many people, too many planes and buses and too much noise this sort of thing had suddenly grown strangely desirable, and he had sat in the boat, feeling drowsiness steal over him in the heat until he had very gently and agreeably fallen asleep.

Now suddenly there had been a monstrous change. The hills had disappeared behind the Letir-Falloch marina. At least he thought it was in the direction of the Letir-Falloch marina, but without the distant view of masts and buildings it was difficult to be sure which direction was which. And the sun had gone in and the wind was raising little ripples on the water. The water itself had changed colour from blue green to steely grey and now looked a great deal less inviting and pleasant than it had done earlier.

The sail lay where he had dropped it in an untidy heap at the foot of the mast. He looked at it uncertainly. If he pulled *that* rope it ought to go up again and once it had gone up he could at least head for the shore somewhere, even if it wasn't in the direction of Letir-Falloch. There was no need to panic. But suddenly the thought of safety on dry land was infinitely desirable.

He crawled clumsily towards the rope he had in mind, finding the boat a great deal less steady than it had been. He didn't dare stand up in case it suddenly decided to pitch him overboard. He knew from having trailed his hand lazily in the water on his way out that in spite of the sun shining so brilliantly on it it was very cold indeed.

He seized the rope and pulled. The sail stirred and moved and he pulled again, feeling the boat rocking uneasily under him as he did so. The sail seemed to meet some sort of obstruction, and he paused to take a better grip of the rope.

As he did so he glanced round again. On all sides the shore had now disappeared into a sort of grey, hazy blanket which seemed to be creeping inevitably towards him across the water. He shivered again, not altogether with the cold, and bent to the rope with renewed vigour. Suddenly the obstruction must have given way and the sail shot up the mast, almost overbalancing him with its suddenness, and he wound the rope clumsily round a metal thing which seemed to be designed for the purpose and tied it in a safe knot.

As he did so a gust of wind seemed to hurtle out of nowhere, struck the sail and made the boat heel suddenly to one side and water came over the edge and lay slopping around the bottom.

He looked at it and felt his heart thumping. Water outside the boat was one thing. Water inside was quite another. It was a great deal too close for comfort. What had started out as a pleasant little trip in the sunlight had turned into something of a nightmare, and a nightmare from which he was not sure if he could waken.

The water was becoming choppier by the minute. The uneasy pitching of the boat became more pronounced and his stomach was beginning to move in sympathy. He remembered the man at the jetty saying that the weather was going to break down and he remembered his own amusement at the idea that it could do so. He wished he'd paid more attention to the man now.

Another, fiercer gust of wind caught the sail and he watched in horror as the mast leant over lazily against the grey sky and almost touched the surface of the loch. A slate-grey comb of water lapped lazily over the edge and came aboard almost reluctantly, filling the bottom of the boat further, and automatically he moved his feet to avoid getting them wet.

And the boat was moving now, gathering way with the wind, but moving hesitatingly, uncertainly, questing here and there as though seeking the right direction.

And then the rain began to fall, and as it did so the world contracted frighteningly into a small circle in which there was only him, the boat, the rain and the hungry water. He searched frantically on all sides for a sign of the shore. But it had disappeared. He had suddenly become cocooned in a wet grey blanket cut off from the rest of the world and from which there seemed to be no escape.

3

The trees were stirring uneasily and it was as though someone had turned the knob on a television set from colour to black and white, MacAulay thought, so the camera round his neck remained in its case. He had hoped to use it, and had he been half an hour earlier would undoubtedly have done so, but now the weather was too dull to get clear, sharp pictures, and as he hoped he would be here for a few more days there was always the chance that conditions would improve again and enable him to get what he wanted.

The churchyard was neat and well kept, the gravestones standing in quiet, ordered ranks, like soldiers on eternal sentry duty.

The weather-beaten, moss-covered names had called to him across the years with mute appeal, carrying with them the customary heartbreak of such places, names of sons dead in war, of daughters dead in infancy, of wives dead in childbirth, of grieving husbands, fathers, mothers. Nothing unusual. You could find the same anywhere in the world, but no less poignant for all that.

There were Peddies galore, the owners of Glendarroch, from the fairly recent Sir Logan Peddie stretching back to the indecipherable Peddies of a couple of centuries back, to the age when gravestones had first appeared as man strove to find a permanent record of his sojourn on earth to leave for the future.

There were Lachlans and Blairs and Craigs and Lamonts and Murdochs and there were MacAulays, whose stones he found just as the rain began to fall and he decided to save them for better weather and hurried to take shelter in the church porch.

The wind gusted heavily sometimes, and he watched the trees bending as though in pain, but he was sheltered here and he was in no hurry to get back to the car, though he wasn't quite sure what his next move should be.

There came the clatter of a bucket from round the corner of the church and a figure appeared hurrying to the porch through the curtain of rain, a figure in a shapeless raincoat with what looked like an upturned pot on its head surmounted by a plastic covering to save it from the rain, and carrying a bucket full of cleaning implements in its hand.

It headed towards him, head down against the wind, and only became aware of his presence as it gained the shelter of the porch and almost cannoned into him, whereupon it raised its head, gave a gasp of surprise and revealed itself to be a woman of indeterminate age and apparently uncertain temper who regarded him as though it were his fault for causing her shock.

"Pardon me, ma'am," he said. "I didn't mean to startle you."

She breathed heavily for a moment and then said, "I have come to clean the church," rather as though she suspected him of having dirtied it on purpose.

"Indeed? And a very worthy object, I'm sure," he said.

She looked at him suspiciously as though unsure whether he were joking or not.

"What are you doing here?" she demanded.

"Sheltering from the rain, ma'am. I was endeavouring to take some photographs when the weather interrupted me."

She sniffed as though the taking of photographs was a frivolous pursuit unworthy of serious folk.

"There are some beautiful headstones here," he added.

"Indeed there are," she said as though he had suggested the exact opposite. "Some very fine Works of Art. And none better, I may say, than that of my Mr Mack who lies just over there."

"Indeed? I should be most interested to see it when the weather improves. Your late husband, ma'am?"

"Yes. People say that it is the best tended grave in the churchyard. Of course, I look after it myself."

"Naturally."

The suspicion which had faded slightly during this excursion to the grave of Mr Mack returned.

"You are an American," she said as though accusing him of some dreadful crime.

"Yes, ma'am."

"Recently arrived here?"

"Yesterday, ma'am."

"Indeed? You are not the person who is staying at Letir-Falloch?"

"Unfortunately no, ma'am. I am staying at the Auchtarne Arms."

"H'm. Then it was not you in the car yesterday with the man Sneddon and Mrs Shaw."

He became alert.

"No, ma'am. I'm afraid not. Who is Mrs Shaw?"

"You may well ask. Mrs Shaw, apart from being the wife of the present owner of the estate, is a nobody. A most forward hussy and not the sort of person who should be living in a place like Letir-Falloch. There are things I could tell you about Mrs Shaw —"

"But Mrs Shaw is here at the moment?"

"Indeed she is. I saw her with my own eyes. In a car. With a man. This, of course, is no surprise to me. I would expect nothing else. Why, the last time she was here —"

And she launched into a hair-raising story which said more for the state of her mind than for factual record and MacAulay took a deep breath. This was his first stroke of luck. Although this woman seemed reluctant to believe it, the man was more than likely to be the owner of Letir-Falloch, and if that were the case he might not need to go very far to find the person who could give him permission to search on Letir-Falloch land.

4

The rain blattered against the window, trying to force its way in and, having failed, subsided in long tears down the glass.

Sally stood watching it, her mind a prey to conflicting thoughts.

Why were things so complicated? Why couldn't they be simple and straightforward?

She tried to sort out her mind which over the past year or so seemed to have become a raging inferno of contradictions.

First there was Harry's American tour. He hadn't wanted her to go with him. He'd wanted to be free with the backing group and the boys, didn't want the encumbrance of a wife with him. She knew from others how an American tour was a time of enormous excitement and almost total licence. The sky was the limit, there were drink, drugs and girls ready and available all the time. And while she was pretty certain he wouldn't take to the drugs because he had more common sense than that, the temptation would be there and the pressure might get to him and she wouldn't be around to advise caution.

And he had sent her here to this newly aquired property which he had never visited and had never intended to, left her in the charge of Sneddon whom she had grown to hate as did most other people in Glendarroch and Auchtarne, Sneddon who had been appointed to the job by Charlie Davenport, which was no kind of recommendation. She liked Charlie Daveport even less than Sneddon because he was unconcerned about anyone or anything except his own pocket. They made a pretty pair, and it was a pity that Harry had fallen so much under the influence of the one and might soon fall under the influence of the other. She wondered how much sending her here had been Harry's idea and how much Charlie Davenport's. Maybe it was purely Harry's and maybe he had believed that here she would be safe from the temptations which he was willingly facing himself.

But there had been temptation. There had been Jimmy Blair, and her heart still felt the ache which had come when they had parted.

She had known that the affair wasn't one which could last. They had both known that and perhaps that was why there had been so much desperation and desire and despair in it during its fragile existence. But it had brought inevitable heartbreak too. And not just for them. Actions could never be seen in isolation. Others had inevitably been drawn in as well. There had been Jimmy's break with Marion for which she felt responsible but powerless to avoid. And such a nice girl, the Mrs Macks had enjoyed informing her. So unassuming, so kind, so *good*. It had all been enough to make Sally hate this Marion whom she had never met, but she hadn't been able to. She had pitied her while at the same time she had pitied herself. And there was the pain the relationship had brought his parents. And there was the worry that Harry should hear about it from Sneddon. But Sneddon had never said. Not so far, anyway. Sneddon obviously wanted it as a hold over her.

It had been passionate, wholehearted and hopeless from the start. Romeo and Juliet stuff, totally unrealistic. And as the unrealism had grown so had their need for each other as though passion could smother the hopelessness of it all, and that was why she had put off for weeks the idea of writing to Harry telling him that she wanted a divorce.

She had never written. And when the cable came to say that he was lying sick in a hospital in Los Angeles she had gone to him immediately.

Why? She had told Jimmy time and time again that everything there had ever been between Harry and her was over. And she had believed that. She had, so far as she knew, been honest. And yet Harry needed her and she had gone to him as a mother to her child and she had brought him home and she still thought of him as her child, her helpless, wounded child who needed comfort and encouragement.

She hadn't needed Harry as she had needed Jimmy.

But sharing a life with someone, first as childhood

sweethearts and then in marriage for seven years, couldn't be cast aside as easily as that. And she hadn't told Harry about Jimmy. When they had got back to London and Harry had suddenly, right out of the blue, announced his intention of coming to Letir-Falloch, the place which he had said he would never go to because there was nothing there for him, she had been shocked and worried. She had protested that she didn't wanted to come and he, disappointed, had asked her why. Her excuses had been lame because she couldn't tell him the real reason and he had pooh-poohed them and as he had obviously set his heart on coming and in view of the state of his health she had given in, albeit reluctantly. She could understand only too well his change of heart. Letir-Falloch was a symbol of peace and quiet, of relief from the strain he had been under during the tour, a chance to get right away from the whole pop business. But at Letir-Falloch and at Glendarroch and at Auchtarne there were people who were only too well aware of her relationship with Jimmy. True, there would be no Jimmy, because she knew he had left at the same time as she had. But memory remained behind, and she knew that it would not be long before someone, either inadvertently or with malice aforethought, told Harry about it.

She would have to tell him herself, but the matter was delicate. Harry had come to rely on her very heavily during the last few weeks, and although his health was improving rapidly, she did not want to cause a setback by telling him that while he had been away she had been unfaithful to him, that it had been many times, and in this very house, and that it had been an experience different from any she had ever known with him, infinitely more glorious, infinitely more distressing.

But she would have to. Over the last few days it had been born in on her that she had to be honest with him, that if they were to have any sort of existence together it could only be on the basis of trust, and she found herself to her surprise longing for that situation, longing for them to be together again as they had been when they were at school and had first got married — far too young, of course — and before Harry hit the big time and had given up the safety of his job as an electrician and grasped the opportunity which seemed to be opening out before him.

Where was he? He had said he was going down to the marina. Did that mean he had taken a boat out? And if he had why was she so desperately worried now? Was it purely maternal?

Another blatter of rain hit the window and the trees beyond the drive writhed and twisted.

She turned and left the room, crossed the hall and opened the door to the office. Sneddon was sitting at the desk, immersed in papers.

"I'm going down to the marina," she said.

"Okay," he said without looking up.

The minimum of conversation which was all she ever held with him nowadays.

She let herself out by the back door and ran for the stables where the Panda was kept as the wind caught her hair and the rain lashed at her face. For some reason she felt such urgency in her that she had not even stopped for a coat.

5

When the front door bell rang Sneddon was in the middle of some complicated calculations concerning the amount of feed he would need to buy in for the Home Farm the following winter. Normally the housekeeper would answer it, but the old bag was still on holiday and there was no one else but himself now that Shaw's wife had gone out.

He flung down his pen in disgust and strode out of the office, across the hall, and opened the front door. A blast of wind hit him as he did so, and beyond he could see the rain falling almost horizontally.

Standing on the doorstep was the same American he'd hurried off the estate the day before.

"What do you want now?" he demanded.

"I should like to see Mrs Shaw, please," said the American.

"Mrs Shaw's not here."

"Pardon me, sir, but I understand that Mrs Shaw is in residence."

"Listen, chum, Mrs Shaw may be in residence, as you put it, but she sure as hell isn't in the house at the moment."

"Then perhaps I may wait for her," said the American.

"Certainly you may wait for her. I can't stop you. But you can do it outside," said Sneddon as the man made a movement as though to step into the house.

Unfortunately he could see the man's car standing outside on the forecourt, so the entertaining thought that he might have to stand out in the rain till Mrs Shaw came back lost some of its charm.

"I see. And when do you expect her back?"

"God knows. She's gone to look for her husband who may be drowned in the loch for all I know. Now, if you don't mind I have work to do —"

"Her husband is here too?"

Dammit, he hadn't meant to admit that.

"Yes, he is."

"Well now, that's even better. Then I shall return at some more convenient time to see them."

"Please yourself. But if you're going to sit in your car and wait for them you may have to wait a long time. And if you do sit there I want to see you *in* the car, and not wandering round on the loose where I can't keep an eye on you. Understand?"

"I understand perfectly, sir. And I shall not cause you unnecessary work by having to keep an eye on me. I shall leave the estate and return at a more convenient time. Good morning."

Sneddon watched as he hurried out to the car, started it, and drove off, before he closed the front door and returned to the office, irritably realising that he had lost count of his calculations and would have to start them all over again.

6

Peter Craig put down the binoculars. It was hopeless. All he could see through them was enlarged raindrops. He

turned away from the window of the marina office,
biting his lip.

That crazy idiot — out there in the boat, without the
savvy to come in when the weather began to turn sour!
What sort of a fool was he? He hadn't looked very
experienced when he set off, almost as though he didn't
really know what a boat was. And he hadn't even put on
his lifejacket.

Craig felt more worried about that fact than any
other. He should have made sure the man had it on
before he left. He had been guilty of a basic failure in his
duty.

He threw himself into the chair at the desk and stared
unseeingly at the photographs of proud yachts
ploughing their way through steep seas with laughing,
toothy young men and girls leaning happily out of them
and wondered what was happening out there on the
loch.

Everyone else was in and accounted for. Everyone else
had behaved sensibly and caused no problems. There
always had to be one. From the neighbouring clubhouse
came the sound of disco music and laughter from all
those who had come in, now warm and happy and dry
and uncaring about the conditions on the loch.

All except one. What should he do now?

He got up and walked restlessly round the office. The
barometer had stopped falling and was now steady. If
the forecast was anything to go by it should start rising
again and the weather should clear within the next hour
or so, and although they might not regain the blazing
sunshine of the last week for a while the wind should
drop and the temperature remain steady.

The door slammed open against the wind and a girl
stood there, hair plastered over her face in rats' tails.

"My husband's out there," she said without any pre-
liminaries, and Craig sighed inwardly. It was bound to
happen, but he wished it hadn't been quite so soon.

"Mrs Grant?" he asked.

"No. Shaw."

"Shaw . . .?"

It was only then that he recognised her. The wet hair
had changed her. Of course. Sally Shaw. The one who

had had that torrid affair with Jimmy Blair.

"He told me his name was Grant," he said accusingly, and then another penny dropped. He had thought the man's face had been vaguely familiar. "But he's not . . . He's — he's Vincent!"

"Yes."

"But he — he signed for the boat — there —" he pointed it out "— as Bernard Grant."

"It's a name he often uses. Then people sometimes don't recognise him. Has he come back?"

Craig stared at the fake signature, suddenly feeling cold. This wasn't any old nobody who was out there on the loch. This was a VIP.

"No. I'm afraid he hasn't," he said. "Not yet."

"Oh, God —!"

"Now, don't worry. It's not all that bad. Even a beginner should be able to handle those conditions without too much trouble. He'll be wet and cold, no doubt —"

"You don't understand. He's not even a beginner."

Craig grew even colder. This was what he had feared at the back of his mind and had desperately fought to keep there.

"He's not?" he said.

"No. So far as I know he's never even taken a rowing boat out on a pond before."

Craig stared at her in disbelief. This was even worse than he had imagined.

"You're sure?" he asked.

It was a silly question and it was treated with the contempt it deserved.

"Of course I'm sure!" she said. "He doesn't know what he's doing."

Craig took a deep breath and reached for the telephone.

"What are you going to do?" she asked, and he could hear the fear in her voice.

"There's only one thing I can do," he said, and began dialling, his finger fumbling in the number holes with the urgency of the occasion.

7

He had been neglecting the books for a week or two because it had been more important to make the actual deliveries of peat, so he was determined that this morning he would catch up on it and put it out of the way before it got totally out of hand.

It wasn't a job Brian enjoyed very much, but it had to be done and, like everything else he touched, it had to be done properly and carefully so that no authority anywhere would have cause to complain or question and have him put back in jail again. That prospect was always hanging over him like the sword of Damocles, and all he could do was make sure the sword never had a chance to fall.

He was working in the back shop because in the living room there would be too many temptations to stop doing what he had to do. Things like easy chairs and television sets and even a window to look out of. Here he was making good progress amongst the unopened packages of goods for the shop, finding the constant sound of movement and of voices from the shop itself acted as a spur to his concentration rather than an intrusion upon it.

Even when the telephone rang in the shop he had no premonition of trouble, scarcely hearing it against the background of all the other noises.

It was only when Isabel poked her head through and spoke to him that he suddenly grew alert.

"It's Eddie for you, Brian. From the lifeboathouse."

He sprang to his feet and went through into the shop and seized the receiver from her, seeing the worry in her face as he did so. She knew as well as he did what this sort of call meant.

"Eddie?" he said.

Eddie's voice came through terse with urgency.

"Brian — there's just been a call from the marina. A sailing boat missing on the loch. Can you crew for me?"

"There in one minute," he said and slammed the receiver back in its rest.

He squeezed past Isabel at the cash register and rounded the counter.

"Boat missing on the loch," he said. "Back soon."

There was no logical reason why he should say that. He didn't know any more than she did how soon or how late he would be back, but it was meant as reassurance.

Then he was out in the wind and the lashing rain and racing for the jetty, the sight of Isabel's worried face firmly imprinted on his mind.

8

"The lifeboat'll be on its way in a couple of minutes," said Craig, putting the receiver back on its rest.

She looked at him expressionlessly.

"Does it know where to go?" she asked.

He wished she didn't have this ability to go straight to the heart of the matter. It was very difficult to be re- assuring in such circumstances.

"I gave them the last known position before the weather closed in," he said.

"You saw him yourself?"

Craig avoided her eye. He couldn't be sure. The last time he had looked there had still been a number of craft out there. He couldn't be absolutely certain which one was Shaw's.

He didn't answer the question directly.

"They know where to look," he said.

"I hope you're right."

She had refused to sit down and she looked awkward and uncomfortable as she stood in the centre of the office, hands clasped in front of her, rain still dripping from the end of her hair. The silence grew and stretched.

"If they find him will they bring him back here?" she asked at last, and he answered eagerly, relieved by the opportunity to break that silence which had seemed to hold accusation in it.

"I don't think so. The wind will be dead against them, so they'll probably head back to Glendarroch," he said.

"I'll go and wait there then."

"A good idea," he said with relief that he would be rid of her presence. "There'll be people at the lifeboat- house."

"I know," she said shortly and turned to leave.

At that moment the door opened and Sneddon came in.

"What's going on?" he asked, and Craig wasn't sure whether he was speaking to him or to her.

"Harry's out on the loch. Alone. In a boat," she said.

He frowned and glanced out of the window before he grunted.

"Should be all right," he said.

"That's what I was saying," said Craig.

"Should be. *Should* be. But *is* he? I'm going to Glendarroch to wait there."

She blundered out past Sneddon into the rain and wind which now seemed to be dropping a little.

Craig said nothing because there didn't seem to be anything to say.

"What the hell did you let him go out for?" Sneddon demanded.

"I didn't know who he was," said Craig.

"Everyone knows who he is," said Sneddon. "Bloody pop star. Top of the charts. Twice. How could you miss him?"

"Look, I'm not exactly a fan. He asked for a boat. Why should I try to stop him?"

"Couldn't you see he was no damned good with the thing?"

"Yes, I could, but by the time I could see that he was out from the jetty and there wasn't anything I could do."

"You try to call him back?"

"No."

"Why not?"

"Well, he seemed quite happy —"

"God — you got that lifeboat on the job?"

"Yes."

"He should be all right then."

"I wouldn't be too sure of that."

"Why not?"

"When I last saw him he wasn't wearing a lifejacket, and if he handles that the way he handled the boat I shouldn't think he'll know how to put the thing on."

Sneddon stared at him expressionlessly for a long time and then swung away to the window and they stood

looking out over what they could see of the loch, where
the waves were wearing white crests now and the rain
still formed an impenetrable curtain.

9

Eddie had the lifeboat out of the lifeboathouse and
halfway down to the water on its trolley by the time
Brian appeared, hurried into the lifeboathouse to grab
the yellow oilskins and lifejacket hanging on a peg
behind the door and then ran to help manoeuvre the
unwieldy contraption into the loch at the side of the
jetty. Nothing was said. It was a well-practised routine.
Once in the water the lifeboat lost its unwieldiness as it
met its natural element, and they floated it off the trolley
and clambered aboard.

The lifeboat was an inflatable with a powerful
outboard motor, nothing like a floating gin palace and
with no semblance of comfort or protection from the
elements, but it was not designed for pleasure cruising.
It was designed for one purpose: that of saving life
quickly and efficiently and for that Eddie had the utmost
respect for it.

He started the outboard and a minute later, while
Brian was still strapping on his lifejacket, they roared off
from the shore, the motor shattering the peace which
had been reigning till then.

The lifeboat lifted its bows clear of the water as they
reached full speed and the spray rose on either side of
them and fell away behind.

It was like heading hell-for-leather into a wet blanket.
Eddie found his eyes narrowed, not against the wind and
spray, but against the thought of something unexpected
tearing into them out of the curtain of rain and mist.
Nothing would, he knew. But visibility was so bad, only
about twenty yards, that he would have virtually no
reaction time if it did.

But visibility seemed to have improved marginally
once they cleared the shelter of the headland and the
lifeboat began to meet the waves. They sat there feeling
as though someone had taken a hammer and was

wielding it against the bows of the boat, determined to prevent them from making progress. It was enough to shake a man into a jelly, Eddie thought, and wondered as he often did how the men of the Royal National Lifeboat Institution could use boats like this in the open sea where the conditions were infinitely worse than they were here.

"Where are we heading?" Brian shouted above the roar of the engine, crouched beside him and holding grimly to a lifeline.

"Peter Craig said the last reported position was about half a mile due west of the marina and the boat seemed at anchor then. We don't know what's happened since."

"How long ago was that?"

"About twenty minutes."

"Could have drifted quite a distance by now."

"I know. We'll get to the position and try a square search. It's all we can do."

"How many aboard?"

"Just one."

The lifeboat bounded forward, shaking their bones apart, and the conversation lapsed. It was far too difficult to try to continue it in the circumstances. Eddie thought there couldn't be a more uncomfortable means of progress over water, but it was fast and it was safe — so long as you hung on — and that was what mattered.

The mist and rain parted ahead of them, tearing past them in shredded tatters, and then closed in again behind them and with one eye on the compass Eddie estimated where they were. It was not easy with no sight of land now to help them pinpoint their position.

"Do it by guess and by God," he said, more to himself than to Brian, but Brian heard him and grinned in sympathy.

They lapsed into silence again. The sound of the engine seemed to reverberate against the wall of mist on all sides, and at last Eddie felt they must have reached the general area where the casualty ought to be. He slackened speed and the roar of the engine subsided to an angry bellow.

As he did so the lifeboat sank its bows into the loch again and they could relax a little as the movement became less violent though just as awkward as more of the hull came in contact with the water.

Then they began the search. A quarter of a mile north, a right angle turn, a quarter of a mile east, a right angle turn, a quarter of a mile south, a right angle turn and a quarter of a mile west with a pause at each turn when they stopped and allowed the engine to idle in the hope that they might pick up a cry for help over the lessened noise.

Nothing.

So start another square. A quarter of a mile east, right angle turn . . .

And the weather began to clear. The second time they turned from north to west they were both aware that the wind in their faces was much less strong than it had been the first time. And as the wind dropped the rain lessened and as the rain lessened the visibility lifted, first to fifty yards, then to seventy, then to a hundred . . .

The waves stayed, though, slapping angrily at the material of the hull, slopping inboard so that Brian had to keep bailing and trying to look through the mist at the same time.

"There!" he shouted, and Eddie followed his pointing finger.

A hundred and fifty yards ahead on the port bow there was something in the water. It swam in and out of the edge of visibility and was difficult to see clearly, but it didn't look like a boat . . .

Eddie increased speed and the lifeboat surged forward, heading for the point.

It was a boat all right, but it was hull up, and he felt his heart miss a beat. The hull looked frighteningly smooth.

He swung round the hull and breathed a sigh of relief. A figure in a soaked white short-sleeved shirt and water-logged red trousers clung desperately to it, hands still managing to grip the ridge of the keel.

"I'll go straight in," he called, and Brian nodded and made his way forward by means of the safety line, ready to lift the man out of the water.

Eddie brought the lifeboat gently in towards the hull and watched Brian signalling from the bows. A bit more . . . Port a little . . . Bit more . . . Bit more . . . Hold her there!

Eddie played with the gears and the rudder, delicately holding the lifeboat in as near the same position relative to the hull as he could. He watched as Brian bent overboard, heard muffled words of encouragement and then there was a heave and the man arched over the curve of the bow to lie across it, gasping for breath. Brian pulled himself back into the lifeboat again and then helped the man fully in as Eddie reversed away from the hull and turned for Glendarroch.

By now the land was visible again, the weather clearing as quickly as it had deteriorated, and he could see where he was going. With the wind and set of the waves astern the run was smoother and he had time to cast an anxious eye at the casualty.

Dressed only in shirt and trousers and without a lifejacket the man had been totally exposed in very cold water for perhaps as much as twenty minutes, and he watched as Brian took off his own oilskin jacket and wrapped it round him. The man nodded his gratitude and as he did so Eddie recognised him. It was Sally Shaw's husband. Harry Shaw. The singer, Vincent. Even with his hair plastered over his face and that face mottled red and white with the action of wind and water, he was plainly recognisable.

Well, well. Local boy rescues famous pop star, he thought. Maybe make the front page of the *Daily Record*.

"All right?" he called.

Brian nodded.

"He's fine," he said. "Cold and wet, but no harm done. A hot drink and dry clothes and he'll be as right as rain tomorrow."

"Don't talk about rain," said Harry Shaw between chattering teeth and Eddie grinned. Quite clearly he was all right.

There was a reception committee waiting for them at the jetty as he brought the lifeboat in. In the lee of the land the waves were virtually non-existent. Sheila was there, of course, as she always was when he had to take the lifeboat out, and there were several locals who always seemed to congregate on these occasions, ready to help, anxious for the safety of the boat they had worked so hard to buy and for their own people who were manning her.

And there was Sally Shaw, pale and tense and untidy.

He brought the lifeboat in and Brian jumped out with a mooring line and then got back in again to help Harry Shaw out.

Sally came running down the jetty and threw herself into his arms.

"You fool!" she said, tears streaming down her face. "You damned silly fool! What did you want to go and do a thing like that for? What were you trying to do to me?"

"Hey, it's all right," he said. "I'm okay. Don't worry."

He kept his arm round her waist as he turned to Eddie.

"Listen, I don't know what to say. There isn't anything really, is there? Thanks just isn't enough."

"It's all right," said Eddie. "Just part of the job."

"Just part of the job, the man says. You just saved my life, in case you hadn't noticed. I couldn't have held on to that boat much longer. And I can't swim . . . I don't know—" He frowned momentarily and then went on with a great air of seriousness — "I don't know what I can do about that."

"Have a few sailing lessons before you do it again, and next time wear a lifejacket," said Eddie.

Harry stared at him for a moment, fighting indignation, then he relaxed with a wry smile.

"Fair enough," he said. "You're right. And so's this one." He squeezed Sally to him as he said it. "I was a fool. And I'm making you all wet."

"I'm all wet already, you dope," she said.

He turned back to Eddie.

"I'll not do it again," he said.

Sally took Eddie's hand and squeezed it.

"Thank you, Eddie," she said. "I'll get him home and dried out. Thanks."

"He'll be fine in a couple of hours, but you could always get Dr Wallace to have a look at him if you like."

"I don't need a doctor. Just some heat," said Harry, and Eddie watched as Sally guided him away from the jetty and put him with motherly care into the passenger seat of the Panda. Then she came round and got into the driver's seat herself and a little later the car headed away from the jetty and up to the road.

He felt an arm on his elbow and turned to look into a pair of very serious and very worried blue eyes.

"You all right?" Sheila asked, and he put his arm round her as Harry had put his round Sally and pulled her to him, feeling the tension which was always present on a rescue like this drain out of him at the touch of her.

"He did a great job," said Brian. "Who knows, we'll make a coxswain of him yet."

"I'd really rather you didn't," said Sheila with a half laugh and a half sob.

"No. Perhaps not. Next thing he'd have his eye on the QEII."

The lifeboat was already being lifted out of the water and replaced on its trolley by the shore helpers.

"She took quite a pounding on the way out. We'd better give her a good looking over," said Eddie as they began to wheel her up towards the lifeboathouse.

"She'd better be all right. We can't afford to repair her again," said Brian.

"Pardon me, sir," said an American voice, and turning, Eddie found himself facing a tall, elderly, gangling man with a stoop. "I hesitate to take up your time when you have just been engaged on a most meritorious act of rescue, but that lady who left in the car just now. Was that Mrs Shaw?"

"Yes, it was," said Eddie.

"And the man with her?"

"Her husband."

"And he is all right, is he?"

"He's fine, yes. But there may be a reaction of some kind. There usually is. He'll probably need rest and quiet for a day or two."

"A day or two?" The man frowned. "I see . . . Thank you, sir. I am very much obliged."

And the stranger turned and walked away. Eddie stared after him. It was almost as though he were disappointed.

Chapter Three

1

There was still a square of daylight at the window when he emerged from a doze and felt Sally slip into bed beside him. He had drifted gently off, warm and comfortable, feeling that the adventure of the morning had in some strange way driven the remembrance of America from his mind. The thought of the tour no longer filled him with fear and foreboding. This morning something more immediately dangerous and frightening had come between him and it. Put it in a proper perspective, perhaps.

He didn't know what time it was and didn't really care.

He'd gone up early, about ten, leaving Sally sitting in that huge drawing room along the corridor by herself, a rather lonely, forlorn figure. Funny. He hadn't thought of her that way before. He wondered why he should suddenly do so now.

"Are you awake, Harry?" she whispered suddenly.

He grunted.

"Can I talk?"

He grunted again, this time in assent.

"Because I've got to," she said.

She lay there silent for a while and when he put a hand across her he felt her body rigid beside him.

He came fully awake.

"What's up?" he asked.

The rigidity finally got through to him. He realised that ever since the accident that morning she had been on the edge of some kind of crisis, and something told him that that crisis was about to be resolved.

"There's something you've got to know," she said, and he heard the quiver in her voice. He thought about putting on the light so that he could see her face, but he knew instinctively that she had chosen this moment so that he couldn't look at her, that she didn't want him to be able to see her, and that seemed to indicate that she felt guilty about something.

"Okay. Fire away," he said.

She was silent for a long time and he wondered if she were having second thoughts, but then she drew a deep shuddering breath and spoke again, keeping her voice calm and quiet with an obvious effort.

"I was going to tell you this anyway. Sometime. When you were better and stronger. I want you to know that. And I want you to believe it. I'm not telling you because I've *got* to so that I can avoid trouble. I'm telling you because I *want* to. But I knew that when you decided to bring me back here with you you'd find out sooner or later and I didn't want you to hear it all wrong."

"What is this?" he asked feeling tension creeping into him from her, and already having an inkling of what it might be about.

"Please. Let me tell it in my own way."

"Sure. Take your time. Some kind of confession, is it?"

"Yes."

He lay silent, listening to the faster breathing beside him. She was in distress and that distressed him.

"Go on, Chicken," he said gently.

She turned away from him suddenly.

"Don't call me that," she said and there was a sob in her voice.

It was one of those stupid names which had grown between them over the years, going back to the first time they had met. It had been the first day at secondary and the two of them had been with a gang of other eleven-year-olds, working their way slowly homewards from school. Being the first day of the first year there was no boring homework to do so there was nothing to hurry for. Their path had taken them along the bank of the canal. Some of the boys had found a broken packing case floating at the edge of the green and scummy water. They had started to dare the girls to cross to the other side on it, laughing and nudging each other as they did so. He'd hardly noticed Sally amongst the girls. She had been small and shy and insignificant and not really worthy of attention and he didn't know why he suddenly turned to her and challenged her to try the crossing. Maybe simply because she *was* small and shy and insignificant and had seemed the most unlikely one to comply and, with the natural cruelty of boys for girls, he had thought that would have been a bigger laugh than actually seeing one of the other girls try it and maybe succeed. She had shaken her head, her eyes on the broken concrete they were standing on, and he'd said, "You're chicken," and she'd looked up at him, surprised, and said, "No, I'm Sally," and somehow the name Chicken had stuck between them ever since. Gradually, now that his attention had been focused on her, he found that he was paying more and more attention to her, finding that the shyness and timidity actually had a fascination of their own, had aroused a kind of protective instinct in him. He had taken to carrying her books home, feeling warmth at the eyes downcast in gratitude, enjoying the jeely piece with which her mother used to reward him. And there had been occasions when he had found himself fighting bigger boys in the playground because they had laughed and jeered at her, and he had got many a black eye for trying to act like Superman. "Chicken" had been a private and secret thing between them, something which no one else shared, and as something very precious he had used it only rarely as their relationship had developed through those schooldays and afterwards during his apprentice-ship and into what had seemed an inevitable marriage.

He had thought that using it now might help, but apparently it didn't.

It was better to say nothing, so he lay waiting until he heard her turn on to her back again and draw a long sigh.

"Sorry. That was silly. It just — doesn't seem right."

"Why not?"

She didn't answer directly.

"When you went off to America, I — I thought you didn't want me any more. I thought you were tired of me and wanted to be free to enjoy things there."

He said nothing because looking back he realised that there was quite a lot of truth in what she said. Ever since he'd thrown up his job to take to singing full time they had drifted apart.

She had understood his job because being an electrician was within the framework of her experience and she could stay happily in the background. But being thrown into the entertainment business was something else. She hadn't enjoyed it. He remembered many occasions when he had become irritated by her inability to participate in the big parties and way-out publicity stunts. Sometimes he had felt she disapproved of them, whereas now he realised that they simply bewildered her. The American tour had been a wonderful excuse to get rid of her, to free himself from the shackles of her narrowmindedness, as he thought of it. But as the tour had gone on and the pressures had increased he had begun to look on her rejection of the life with a great deal more sympathy.

"You sent me here, and I was alone in this huge house with no one to talk to but that beast Sneddon. Oh, God, you've no idea how lonely it was."

"I didn't know —"

"How could you? You were over there in the middle of a wonderful time. Oh, I know," she went on, drowning his protest. "It wasn't all that wonderful. I know that now. But I thought then that it must be wonderful. And here I was, left behind, not wanted. No friends, nothing to do."

She stopped and he had a sudden picture of what she was talking about. He knew his accountant had bought this white elephant as a tax-loss but that was all it had been. He hadn't known the house, had never even seen the monstrous size of it, the huge echoing rooms and the vast outlying land. He'd just known it as a name on a piece of paper, somewhere where Sally could be put out of his mind and kept out of trouble — and temptation . . .

"Well, I made a friend," she said hesitantly.

"One friend?"

"One particular friend."

There was another silence as he took that in, and the little niggle of doubt which had been in the back of his mind began to grow and take shape.

"Who was he?" he asked.

"He used to run the ferry. His parents keep the local shop in Glendarroch." The words were coming faster now, because she had reached the main hurdle and was anxious to clear it. "His name was Jimmy Blair and we — well, we fell in love."

Four small, simple words, each of one syllable. Harmless little words. He had been expecting them but to hear her say them was like the twist of a knife in his gut.

"Really in love?" he asked after a while, longing for her to say no it was just a momentary infatuation, nothing more.

"Really in love," she said. "I think it was the same for him as it was for me. It was awful. There was no happiness in it for either of us. Dodging people. Guilt. He — well — he had a girlfriend. Before I came. I never met her but she was a real nice girl. People kept telling me how nice she was. All very pointed. She must have suffered. His parents didn't approve. I'm still frightened to go into the shop and face his mother again. Everything about it was wrong. But — we couldn't stop. Couldn't help ourselves. He — he asked me to marry him. Get a divorce as soon as possible and we'd go away somewhere and get married and everything would be all right. I was to write to you to tell you that I wanted a divorce."

"You never did."

"No."

"Why not?"

"I think I knew it wouldn't work. It couldn't work. And maybe I didn't really want a divorce. Not deep down. Then when you got ill I saw where I had to be, so I told — Jimmy that it was no good."

"Where is he now?"

"I don't know. I don't even know if his parents know. I drove him away from them. He left about the same time I did. And that's that."

He lay there taking it all in slowly, feeling the pain at his heart as he did so, the pain and the anger, and he longed to hit out, shout at her, blame her for being loose and faithless and all the rest of the Victorian words, but somehow he couldn't do it.

"Did you — how far did it go?" he asked, although he already knew the answer.

She didn't reply.

"All the way?" he asked.

He felt her head move as she nodded.

"Yes," she whispered.

"Often?"

"Yes."

"How often?"

"Oh, God, I didn't count, Harry! Whenever we could. He needed me and I needed him. I'm sorry. I don't expect you to understand —"

It was almost an invitation to him to say that he did, that he forgave her, but it wasn't as easy as all that, and he wasn't sure yet whether it was true. There was an awful lot to be thought about.

"Would you — would you like me to sleep next door?" she asked at last in a small, timid voice which went to his heart more than anything else had done.

"No," he said. "Stay there. Don't go away."

He sensed her turn to him and heard her sniff wetly.

"Thanks, Harry," she said in a muffled tone of voice. "I don't think I could bear to be alone tonight."

But he didn't turn to her and take her in his arms and kiss away her tears. He turned away from her and lay staring towards the wall of the room, and he thought they might as well have been in separate rooms, alone and apart.

2

"If I've had to straighten out this stanchion once I've had to straighten it out ten times," said Archie in disgust, looking at the metal bar in the vice. "There are limits, you know, Bob, and I think we've just about reached one of them here."

Bob Taylor looked at the stanchion from the lifeboat critically.

"Seems pretty straight to me, Archie," he said.

"Straight? Of course it's straight. Who straightened it? Me. The man with the most accurate eye in the business. Straighteye, they used to call me at school."

"Is that because you only had one?"

Archie looked pained.

"Do you mind?" he asked. "Stick to the point. It's straight enough. But every time it gets bent it weakens the metal. Some day that thing's going to snap, and I just hope it's while it's in the vice here and not when the lifeboat's out on the loch in a howling gale."

It was gloomy in the lifeboathouse for the sun had never broken through this morning. The lifeboat itself sat on its trolley behind them, looking, Archie thought, tired and dispirited, rather as he felt himself.

"It's time we had a new one. In fact it's time we had half a dozen new ones," Archie said.

"Lifeboats?" asked Bob.

"No. Stanchions. Though mind you, a new lifeboat might not be a bad idea."

"Oh, aye?" said Bob. "And what are you going to use for money?"

"That's just it. I don't know. There isn't even money for stanchions."

They had stripped the outboard's framework because during the battering the boat itself had received yesterday one of the stanchions had become bent. It wasn't the first time it had happened, and the trouble was that each time they straightened it, the stanchion bent more easily the next time the lifeboat was out. Yesterday's rescue shouldn't have had any effect on the lifeboat or its gear. Conditions hadn't been all that bad. And it wouldn't have had any effect if all the equipment had been in prime condition.

They worked for a while at the stanchion until they were sure that it was absolutely true and then they removed it from the vice and began to reassemble it at the stern of the lifeboat.

It didn't take long, and Archie straightened up, removed his cap and scratched the back of his head.

"That's just about the best we can do," he said. "It'll have to last till the next dance."

"Eh?" said Bob.

"The next time we try raising money for the lifeboat."

"Not another dance," said Bob.

"Why not?"

"Last time we had a dance I asked Mrs Mack for one and she looked at me as though I'd made an immoral suggestion."

"You're sure it was a dance you asked her for?"

"For heaven's sake, Archie, what else?"

"Only you can answer that. But the thought of you dancing with Mrs Mack is immoral enough. Anyway, have you got any other bright ideas about how to raise money for the lifeboat?"

He wiped his hands on a piece of cotton waste, turned to the door and came face to face with someone standing there. He dropped the cotton waste in surprise.

"Here, you shouldn't do that," he said in protest. "Think of my old ticker. It's not what it used to be."

"Sorry," said the newcomer. "Is Eddie here?"

"No. Eddie'll be in Auchtarne at the moment with the ferry. No one here but us and we're daft," said Archie.

"Can we help?" asked Bob.

"No, it's okay. Thanks all the same."

The stranger turned and the light from the door caught his face. Archie recognised him.

"You're Harry Shaw," he said.

"That's right," said Harry in the tone of voice of one used to being identified.

"I thought so. I saw you here yesterday when they landed you. Pleased to meet you, Mr Shaw. We've just been giving your carriage a service."

"Is it all right?"

"Well, it's as right as we can make it. It's about due for a proper overhaul, but goodness knows when we'll be able to afford that."

"Can we give Eddie a message?" asked Bob.

"No, I just wanted to say thanks properly for yesterday."

"Och, don't bother," said Archie. "He'll only get a swollen head."

"Or the other man with him. I never even found out who that was. The one who actually pulled me in."

"That was Brian. Brian Blair. I don't think he'll be around either. He'll be out making deliveries."

"Brian Blair?" There seemed to be a note of caution in the voice.

"That's right."

"Well, I'll — I'll maybe see them later."

"They'll both be around the village this evening, I should think."

"Okay. Cheerio for now."

Archie watched Harry Shaw walk slowly away, shoulders hunched and head down.

"Know what?" he said to Bob when Harry was out of earshot.

"What?"

"There goes a man with quite a lot on his mind," said Archie significantly.

3

Grace had just given Dougal his potted haugh when the knock came at the door. She clicked her tongue and went to open it and found herself looking up at a tall thin man with thinning grey hair who carried a shapeless floppy greyish hat in his hands.

"Mrs Lachlan?" he asked.

"Aye, that's me," she said.

"I'm pleased to make your acquaintance, ma'am. I wonder now, is your son at home at present? Mr Dougal Lachlan?"

"Well — yes," she admitted.

"Would it be convenient for me to speak with him for a moment?"

Grace hesitated, not because she was unwilling to admit the stranger, but because Dougal was not always at his most polite when he was interrupted in the middle of a meal and besides, Dougal eating was not a pretty sight. However, the man seemed so quiet and courteous that she couldn't very well refuse, and besides it was not in her nature to do so.

"Of course. Come in," she said and stood aside to let him pass into the living room of the croft house.

He sounded as if he were an American, and she wondered what on earth someone like that would want with Dougal.

Dougal was busy at the table, lowering food into himself with the concentration of a man who has been outside for some hours and is now very hungry. He turned, jaws working, as the man came in and looked at him in slow suspicion.

"Mr Dougal Lachlan?" said the stranger.

Dougal thought about it for a moment and then decided to admit it.

"That's me," he said.

"I have interrupted you at your meal. I apologise, sir. Perhaps it would be more convenient if I returned later."

"No, no, that's all right," said Dougal.

"Will you be taking something yourself?" asked Grace, hoping the man would refuse because there was only enough in the pot now for her, but to her relief he shook his head.

"It's a little early for me, ma'am, I thank you. I shall probably return to the Auchtarne Arms for something later on."

"Sit down," she said, indicating Dougal's chair by the fire and the stranger sank into it. It was a low chair and by the time he got there his knees were almost touching his chin.

"You'll take a cup of tea," said Grace.

"Well —"

"Or maybe coffee, seeing you're an American, am I not right?"

The stranger smiled.

"I won't ask how you guessed I'm American," he said. "Tea would be perfect, ma'am, thank you,"

Dougal was regarding him with wary eyes, but not forgetting to down the food on the plate in front of him.

"Was there something I can do for you?" he asked.

"Well, sir, yes. I sincerely hope so," said the stranger. "I have been asking around in Auchtarne and I understand that you probably know these hills and glens better than anyone else in the neighbourhood."

"Aye, that'll be right," said Dougal who didn't believe in false modesty.

"I wonder, sir, if you might be able to guide me over some of the Letir-Falloch land?"

Dougal stared at him for some time.

"Aye, I *could*," he said slowly, "but I'm not sure that I *would*. It would depend on what your reason is, Mr — er —?"

"MacAulay. David MacAulay."

At the sound of the name Grace looked up sharply

from the cooker where she was putting the kettle on the gas.

"MacAulay?" she said.

"Yes, ma'am."

She looked at him in a new light. Sure enough, the height and the thinness of the face made her realise something which ought to have struck her before.

"You must be one of the MacAulays of Letir-Falloch," she said.

His eyes brightened with pleasure.

"The name is not forgotten in these parts?" he said.

"It certainly is not. The name MacAulay means as much round here as Peddie does."

"I really am mighty pleased to hear that. So far no one has reacted to it."

"Have you told folk your name?"

"Well, not often, no. I did mention it at Glendarroch House."

"Aye, Mrs Cunningham would have known it right away, but she's not here just now."

"It was a Miss Cunningham I spoke to."

"Miss Fiona. The name MacAulay doesn't mean so much to the young folk as to us older ones, Mr MacAulay, and of course it isn't all that uncommon a name."

She looked at him, seeing again the family resemblance but as yet unable to reconcile it to the voice.

"You sound American," she said.

"I am American, ma'am."

Grace found her memory going back many years.

"When I was a young girl there were a wheen MacAulays at Letir-Falloch. There was old Mr Douglas and young Mr Douglas. I remember young Mr Douglas's wedding. It was a red letter day in these parts. I couldn't have been more than ten at the time but I remember the whole district was at the reception in the grounds. They were generous folk, the MacAulays. Mercy, what a time ago that is!"

"My uncle, ma'am. He was the elder brother. My father was Malcolm MacAulay."

"Malcolm MacAulay. Would you credit that?" said Grace. "I'd forgotten all about him. But that's no wonder. He emigrated to America, didn't he?"

"That's correct, ma'am. That was in 1920. Two years after the First World War. I reckon things must have been a mite tough for younger sons at that time, and he thought he'd make good in the States. He did too. Got married out there a couple of years after he arrived."

"And you're his son."

"His younger son, ma'am."

"You have a brother?"

"Had. He was killed during the war. In Italy."

"Och, I'm sorry to hear that now. But I thought it was Mr Douglas's son that got killed."

Mr MacAulay nodded.

"They were killed within a year of each other," he said. "My brother James in 1943, young Douglas in Normandy just a year later. The family wasn't touched by the First World War. But their luck ran out in the second. We were hard hit that time round. My uncle, who inherited Letir-Falloch, of course, was left with a daughter, and my father with just the one son."

"The daughter. Astrid MacAulay."

"You've hit it, ma'am. My cousin Astrid. I never saw her, but we corresponded a great deal until a year or two before her death."

"She only died four years ago, and by then most folk had forgotten the MacAulays. She became a wee bit of a recluse in her last years, you see. We never saw her. There were stories about her going out of her mind, but I think the poor soul was just ill. She never married so after she died the estate was put on the market."

"I knew about that. In fact I reckoned I might try to buy it and come back, but — well — what would be the point? The MacAulays are finished, ma'am, let's face it. I have never married and when I go there will be no one left. Besides, coming back would have been too big a break. My life is in America. I'm an American citizen and at my age the thought of throwing all that in and starting again was too much. But I had to take the chance of coming to see the old place while I could still do it."

"And the man Sneddon won't let you see over the estate, is that it?" said Grace.

"Well, I've had a brush or two with him, yes, and I

don't mind admitting I find that gentleman just a mite obnoxious. But I haven't come back just to see the estate and indulge in a little nostalgia."

Grace saw Dougal push his empty plate away and she went to the cooker to get his pudding and make the tea.

"I trained as an archaeologist, ma'am. Most of my work has been on the pre-Columban sites in America. That's where my main interest lies, but I also find a great fascination in the neolithic and bronze ages."

Grace wasn't quite sure what all that meant and Dougal stirred restlessly in his chair as she put the plate down in front of him. She returned to the cooker where the kettle was beginning to sing.

"My father died a little over six years ago and my mother followed him less than a year later. They had been a real devoted couple and I feel sure that she just didn't want to go on living without him. Anyway, the two deaths so close together meant that it was left to me to clear up the debris of two lifetimes. Not a pleasant job."

Grace remembered what she had had to do when her own husband had died and the heartbreak she had experienced at the necessity of disposing of the intensely personal things, the clothes, her old letters, things which had been precious and private between them but meant nothing to others, not even Dougal.

"However, one of the interesting things I found was a bundle of letters which my father had kept from *his* father, old Douglas MacAulay."

Grace nodded.

"I remember him. A fine old gentleman with a bristling moustache and a voice like a bull and as gentle with it as a wee bairn."

"That sounds like him, ma'am, and corresponds to the photographs we had of him. There was much news of Letir-Falloch in those letters and it was while I was reading them that I determined to come here some time whenever I could manage it. But in one of the letters, dated early in 1939, there was a reference to a famous archaeologist of the day who had stayed at Letir-Falloch with a shooting party in the previous fall — autumn I should say — and the fact that he was — blethering? Is that the word?"

"It's a good Scots one," said Grace. "It means talking nonsense."

"Yes. He was blethering about the fact that he was sure there were neolithic remains on the land. I remember the phrase my grandfather used. 'He seems to think we're perched on top of a damned stone age housing scheme,' was how he put it. Now, there is possibly a lot of truth in this. There are many neolithic remains in this part of the country. Bronze Age too. Though a housing scheme is a mite fanciful, I guess. But one thing this archaeologist found when he was out with the shooting party was an indication of a neolithic stone circle on the land and he felt the stone circle could be mighty important."

"A stone circle?" said Dougal in a mystified tone of voice.

"An ancient Stone Age monument. Your Stonehenge is probably the best known stone circle in the world."

"That's in England," said Dougal.

"Indeed it is, sir, but there are others, and quite a few of them are in this part of the country."

"And did he find it?" asked Grace politely. She found it difficult to get excited about stone circles, however old.

"That's the tantalising bit about it, ma'am. The war started and there were more important things to write about than stone circles. It was never mentioned again in any of my grandfather's letters. So you see, I had two reasons for coming here. One was to see the home of my forefathers and the other was to try to locate this mysterious stone circle which was mentioned in my grandfather's letter."

"And the man Sneddon won't let you look at the house or the grounds," said Dougal.

"That is correct. I understand the present owners are at home at the moment, but for various reasons I am unable to visit with them, and Mr Sneddon seems determined that I shan't contact them through him. Now, my time here is not unlimited and I am most anxious to find out about this stone circle as soon as I can. The land is certainly rich in possibilities. I have already located what looks like an undisturbed barrow —

a burial mound," he added hastily as Dougal began to expostulate, probably about to tell Mr MacAulay that there was nothing unusual about a barrow, and that he had one in the byre. "And that was only on my first exploration. If you can help me to get on to Letir-Falloch land to try to find one or two possible locations which I would describe to you, I should be most grateful."

Dougal looked thoughtful for a moment and then grinned.

"You could go yourself, you know," he said. "You don't need me."

"Sorry?"

"You'll be worried about trespassing, I'm thinking."

"Well, yes, I am."

"You needn't be. There's no such thing as trespass in Scotland. So long as you do no damage no one can touch you for being on their land."

"I was not aware of that fact, sir." Mr MacAulay frowned thoughtfully. "What you tell me is heartening," he said at last, "but I would not relish meeting this man Sneddon when he was in a bad temper. I understand he has an unsavoury reputation and I have already been made aware of that personally."

Dougal nodded.

"So you want to get on to Letir-Falloch without him seeing you," he said.

"I think at this stage that would be advisable."

"And you would not be thinking of doing any damage on the land?"

Mr MacAulay smiled at him.

"Certainly not."

"Mphm."

Dougal scraped up the last of the pudding and pushed the plate aside, leaning his head on his chin thoughtfully. Grace set the teapot down on the table, leaving it to mask for a few minutes.

"Of course Dougal will do it, Mr MacAulay," she said.

"It's for me to decide, Mother," said Dougal.

"Dougal, Mr MacAulay is a MacAulay of Letir-Falloch. He has more right to be on that land than the man Sneddon."

"I know that, and I'll do it, but not just for that reason.

I'll do it because I don't like Sneddon and I'd like to get back at him for some of the things he's done to us. How would this afternoon suit you, Mr MacAulay?"

"Admirably, sir. But are you sure that wouldn't be intruding on your valuable time?"

"Not at all. I was going over to the deer farm this afternoon anyway and as luck would have that's just the way I would take to get you into Letir-Falloch."

4

"It's my opinion, Isabel, that the man did not want to be rescued," said Mrs Mack.

Unfortunately the shop was empty and Mrs Mack was full of doom-laden theories and the combination of the two meant that Isabel had had about five minutes of listening to her opinions on everything from the immorality of most of the people of Glendarroch — Eddie and Sheila in particular — to the reasons for the arrival of the Shaws at Letir-Falloch, but this latest one seemed even more ridiculous than most.

"How do you make that out, Mrs Mack?" she asked.

"It seems perfectly straightforward to me. The woman has finally seen the error of her ways. This may have been brought about by her return to the scene of her carnal shame. In any case, in an agony of remorse she has confessed her infidelity and he has been unable to stand living with it."

Isabel suppressed a sigh. She might have known that there would be something personal in Mrs Mack's attack. Sally Shaw had been unfaithful to her husband with Jimmy. That was what she was really saying, of course, only not quite in so many words.

"That doesn't seem very likely to me, Mrs Mack. To take a boat out in beautiful weather in the belief that it was going to blow up rough so that he could be drowned, is that what you mean?"

"We don't know that he wanted the weather to do his dirty work for him. Perhaps he simply meant to jump over the side."

"Perhaps. But if he was wanting to jump into the

water it would have been easier to do it from somewhere like Laird's Point rather than go to the expense of hiring a boat just to jump out of."

"But expense is no object as far as this man is concerned, Isabel. He is what they call a pope singer. And we all know what that means. Sex and drugs and money."

"It sounds a bit far-fetched to me."

"With these people, Isabel, everything is designed for publicity. Taking out a boat and getting drowned from it is much more spectacular than drowning yourself at Laird's Point. Unless, of course," she added with heavy sarcasm, "you are going to issue invitations to Laird's Point for the event."

"If it's publicity you want you could do it from the marina jetty."

"Ah, but there someone might try to stop you."

Once Mrs Mack got the bit between her teeth no amount of common sense would get it out again.

"I still don't think it's likely, Mrs Mack."

"Likely or not, the man might have had more consideration for others. The lifeboat was called out quite unnecessarily and I believe it now needs further repairs which we can't afford. It was extremely thoughtless of him."

"Besides endangering the lives of those who went to rescue him," Isabel reminded her.

Mrs Mack pursed her lips and said nothing for once, but Isabel could see the thought behind her eyes: Brian Blair, a murderer, and Eddie Ramsay, a ne'er-do-weel who had been living blatantly in sin in the middle of the village, were two people who weren't worth saving.

The bell rang as the shop door opened and one of the objects of her strictures walked in.

Isabel had never met Harry Shaw but she had seen his picture often enough in the popular press to know who he was, so she said "Good morning" politely and cautiously and received a polite and quiet "Good morning" in return. He went to the magazine counter and began to look through the stock there, but she got the impression that he wasn't really interested in magazines.

"And how is Jimmy, Isabel?" asked Mrs Mack suddenly and loudly. "Have you heard from him recently?"

"Not for some time, no," said Isabel, hastily totting up Mrs Mack's few purchases and almost grabbing the money from her hand in order to get her out of the shop before she created yet another unpleasant incident. Enquiries for Jimmy inevitably meant some kind of a dig at someone and it was fairly obvious who this one was aimed at.

"Such a pity the lad had to leave home, I always say," said Mrs Mack with patent unctuousness. "It was a most unfortunate affair, wasn't it?"

"That's twenty-seven pence change, Mrs Mack, thank you," said Isabel firmly, pressing the money into her hand.

Then as Mrs Mack opened her mouth to continue her indirect attack on Harry Shaw Isabel took the unaccustomed action of coming round the counter and opening the shop door for her.

"I think it's going to clear up, don't you, Mrs Mack?" she said briskly, saying the first thing that came into her head, anything in order to stop Mrs Mack from talking.

Mrs Mack grunted, cast a withering glance in the direction of Harry Shaw's back and left reluctantly with her shopping bag.

Isabel drew a deep breath of relief and closed the door, returning to the counter.

"Can I help you?" she asked.

He turned to face her. Dark hair, dark haunted eyes, a long nose, narrow chin. Not good-looking at all, but pleasant. Homely. He looked pale, she thought, and rather vulnerable, not at all like the popular image of the great star under the lights on the stage with the hordes of fans screaming approval at him from below. Just like an ordinary boy, rather like Jimmy . . .

"It's Mrs Blair, isn't it?" he said.

The voice was pleasant, with definite Glasgow intonations but not like the raucous noise that the microphones and the amplification reduced it to. She was beginning to realise that the pop star image had nothing whatsoever to do with reality, and that this man here was real.

"That's right," she said.

"I'm Harry Shaw," he said, and then relapsed into silence as though he's said all he'd come to say. She didn't quite know how to reply, so she simply waited.

"Who was that?" he asked, jerking his head at the shop door through which Mrs Mack had just gone.

"Oh, that was only Mrs Mack. She's a lonely soul. You don't want to pay too much attention to what she says."

"Don't I? But she was right, wasn't she?"

"Well —"

"About your son having to leave home, I mean. Because he'd been having an affair with my wife."

Isabel felt her face flush with embarrassment. This was plain speaking with a vengeance. One didn't usually talk quite so openly about such things to perfect strangers.

"I — I think Jimmy was thinking about leaving anyway —" she said inadequately.

"But he didn't go until that happened."

"No."

"You've felt bitter about Sally since then, right?"

This was getting worse and worse. What was he going to do? Hit her for feeling that way about his wife? And yet there was no anger in his voice. There was something else, and it sounded like sorrow.

"Well —" she said, but he saved her in her desperate attempt to find some neutral reply.

"Please, Mrs Blair, will you do me a favour and don't blame her?"

"Well, I've been trying to tell myself that it takes two to get involved that way."

"Aye. Maybe you're right. But whiles it takes three."

"What they call an eternal triangle, you mean?"

"You could say that. I was the other part of it, anyway, and it's me you should be blaming."

"But — you weren't even here."

"No. That's the point. I should have been. I was away in America enjoying myself. I wasn't really. Enjoying myself, I mean. But I thought I was going to and so did most other people. Like Sally. And I should have been here with her. Or maybe she should have been there with me. I thought she'd have hated it, and I still think she would have done. I never thought she'd have hated here just as much. But she did. She told me all about it last night. It wasn't easy for her, but she did tell me."

Isabel looked at him with growing sympathy, and she knew that the sympathy wasn't only for him. Some of the things Jimmy had said and some of the things Sally had said too had made her think that Sally wasn't the scarlet woman Mrs Mack believed her to be and that Isabel herself would have liked her to be.

"That was very brave of her," she said.

"Yes, it was. She's always seemed shy and frightened. But she's really a very brave person. I didn't understand that before. But I do now. And I understand why she was so lonely when she came here and why she needed comfort and help which I should have given her but didn't. Know what? I neglected her."

He was wandering round the shop, not looking at her, fingering some of the stock without seeing it. He wasn't avoiding her eye through guilt, she thought, he was simply trying to work things out in his own mind as he spoke.

"That's why she turned to your son. Don't blame him and don't blame her. Blame me. I'd like to meet him some time. Just to apologise."

"Apologise?"

"Yes. I drove him away from you, didn't I? Drove him out of Glendarroch."

"No, I don't think that's true. As I said, I think Jimmy was already thinking about leaving. He'd got tired of Glendarroch. The lack of jobs. Lack of opportunity. Mrs Shaw was just the last straw," she said.

"Maybe. But it's funny, isn't it? I've been thinking about this all night. The things I did — or didn't do — didn't just affect Sally's life. They affected you and your husband and your son. People I didn't even know existed. That's kind of frightening."

"I suppose it is —"

"So I just want to apologise."

"Och, there's no need for that —"

"Yes, there is. And please. Don't be too hard on Sally. She never meant to hurt anyone, and the one she's hurt most has been herself."

"I don't blame her alone. I blamed her and Jimmy, I suppose," said Isabel, and then feeling that the conversation was becoming a bit tense she tried to lighten it. "Now, if you like, I'll blame you as well and that means all three of you will have a lot to less to bear."

He smiled fleetingly at her, appreciating what she was trying to do.

"Good," he said. "Here, I'm glad I've got that out of the way."

"It was good of you to come, Mr Shaw. And to say what you've said. It couldn't have been easy."

He let his breath out in an exaggerated whistle.

"You can say that again," he said, and he smiled at her, a brilliant, heart-warming smile which faded as quickly as it came. "This is National Apology Week for me, because I'd like to apologise to your husband too."

"Brian?"

"Yes. Your son is his son as well, isn't he?" She nodded mutely. "But I wanted to apologise to him specially for what I did yesterday."

"Oh. In the boat?"

"Aye."

"You didn't go out in it to drown yourself?"

"Not deliberately, no," he said in surprise, "but I damned nearly did it."

"Well, that's a relief," said Isabel cheerfully. "Mrs Mack had it that your wife had confessed to you last night and you couldn't bear it and went out to commit suicide."

Harry stared at her with his mouth open.

"She said that?" he asked.

"Almost her very words."

"Crumbs. Sally was right. Everyone knew about it except me, and it obviously wouldn't have been long before I got told."

"Not long at all with people like Mrs Mack around."

"Well, I didn't mean to drown myself. I just went out without thinking. And I didn't do any of the things I should have done and I fell asleep and got into trouble, and other people had to risk their lives to rescue me."

"Well, that's what we've got the lifeboat for. I'm just

glad it was here. A couple of years ago you might not have been so lucky. You'd be surprised at how many people used to get into difficulties on the loch. And the number was growing. Usually it was because there wasn't a boat fast enough to reach them in time. It's very cold out there —"

"You can say that again."

"Aye, you don't need me to tell you that. And you don't last long before — what is it? — hypo thingummy sets in."

"Thermia, isn't it?"

"Aye, that's it. So we set about trying to buy a lifeboat. It took us quite a long time to raise the money, but we had help and we got it in the end."

"And now you're landed with looking after it."

"Aye, I'm afraid so. It's one thing buying a lifeboat. It's quite another thing keeping it."

"Yes, I know. I want to do something about that."

"Well, people who get rescued often feel they want to make a donation to the lifeboat maintenance fund," said Isabel. "It all helps."

He nodded.

"Aye," he said. "That's the obvious thing to do. The trouble is, writing a cheque is just too easy. I'll have to think about it."

He stood frowning thoughtfully for a minute and she looked at him in a new light. He wasn't just — what was the name he used — Victor? — no, Vincent. That was it. Vincent was just a front, a disguise he obviously put on whenever he stepped on to a stage. He was just an ordinary young man, with a young man's problems and a young man's fears. Just like everybody else, in fact. The only difference was that he had an enormous amount of money. But it said a lot for him that that enormous amount of money didn't seem to have changed the man himself.

"Anyway, thanks for listening to me, Mrs Blair," he said, heading for the shop door. "I'd like to come back some time and see Mr Blair."

"You'd be welcome any time," she said, and she meant it.

5

About a quarter of a mile above the deer fence Dougal began to move with more caution.

"We're just getting on to Letir-Falloch land now," he said, "so keep your eyes skinned for any sign of the man Sneddon."

He glanced at his companion with grudging respect. He had had some doubts about conducting Mr MacAulay into Letir-Falloch, not because he objected to intruding on Letir-Falloch land, but because he was not sure if Mr MacAulay himself were capable of making the long journey over heavy and difficult ground. He was not a young man — Dougal would have put him at the wrong side of sixty — but his wiriness concealed strength and he was clearly in excellent condition. The man was not even breathing heavily.

"You want lower ground, is that right?" said Dougal, and MacAulay nodded.

"Yes," he said. "Neolithic man would never have built as high as this. He would look for low-lying sheltered ground to build on, with protection from rain and cold and wind."

Dougal nodded. MacAulay had been talking on his pet subject all the way up here and Dougal had listened at first with only half an ear, but gradually the man's enthusiasm had affected him too, and he had begun to see the people of those unbelievably far off times as real people not just as objects in a dry history book.

"Well, the house is down there." He pointed. "And I suppose from what you were saying the house would be built on the sort of land you're looking for."

"That is quite correct, Mr Lachlan."

"Och, call me Dougal. Everyone does. When people say Mr Lachlan I look round to see who else is here."

"Very well — Dougal. Thank you. And I would take it as a favour if you would call me David."

"Well, now, why not? But isn't it funny how things change? My father would never have called your father Malcolm. It would have been Mr MacAulay with a tug of the forelock."

"Thank God those days are gone, sir, is all I can say."
Dougal nodded in agreement.

"Aye. I was never very good at tugging a forelock," he
said. "Well, then, I think what you're after is the low
ground behind the house. So I'll take you to the way
down to those parts, and from there you can get to it
without being seen from the house at all."

"You're not coming with me?"

"There's no need. You're good on a hill, David, better
than most I have to take out here whiles, and on the way
down one person is more difficult to spot than two."

"That's true, Dougal. Right. Lead on."

Dougal led the way through the heather across the
shoulder of a hill and found a cleft which started the
downward slope to the low ground. He led the way down
it until the first bushes began to appear and then the first
stunted trees. When he reached this shelter he waited till
MacAulay came up behind him.

"There's your path," he said. "Between those trees
there. A quarter of a mile down you'll find the start of a
wee burn. The path follows it. Keep on it till you reach a
big clearing in the woods. That's where you're heading.
From there on there are flat clearings in different places
all over the ground. You'll know whether the ones you
want are there or not."

MacAulay nodded.

"Thank you," he said. "And getting out again?"

Dougal grinned.

"If I were you I'd wait till the gloaming, then just slip
out past the house, down the drive and on to the road.
Sneddon'll be tucked up with the whisky bottle by half
past eight. Though it means you'll have to hang around
for a few hours yet."

"I reckon I won't weary. In fact I wouldn't be surprised
if there isn't enough time," said MacAulay and he held
out his hand. "Thank you, Dougal. You've been mighty
helpful."

Dougal nodded and shook it and they parted. He stood
for a moment watching with admiration in his eyes as
MacAulay moved quietly and smoothly down the slope
between the thickening trees. It was not just that he
moved so well and seemed so at home on the hill, but the

man hadn't offered him money, and for that Dougal felt a great respect.

6

She had lain awake for hours, not moving, lying on her back staring sightlessly at the delicately moulded ceiling of the room which faded more and more as the light outside dimmed to its lowest summer point. The curtains were closed, of course, and although they were lined the room faced west so it was inevitably light. Beside her she knew Harry was lying awake too, for he was very silent in his breathing and unnaturally still. She longed to be able to touch him, hold him to her as she had done when they were so very much younger, still teenagers the pair of them, seeking and finding mutual comfort from the pressures of an uncaring world. Now that she had probably ruined their relationship for ever, she suddenly realised that she needed him very badly.

She had finally fallen into a deep and unrefreshing sleep as the birds began their dawn chorus outside, and when she dragged herself awake from it, Harry had gone.

The clock on the bedside table said eight o'clock and she wondered how long ago he had slipped out of bed and dressed so quietly that he hadn't disturbed her and left the room.

Had he slept at all?

She forced herself to stay in the room until she heard Sneddon leave the house on his normal daily round of the estate and then she got up and dressed hastily in a shirt and jeans and hurried downstairs. She looked round the kitchen in dread, expecting to see the white square of a note he might have left, saying that he had gone and wasn't coming back.

But that was ridiculous, of course. If he were going to do such a thing he'd have left it in the bedroom, not here where Sneddon would have found it and might even, for all she knew, have opened it.

Anyway, there was nothing and she wasn't quite sure whether she should feel relieved or more worried.

She made a cup of tea and drank about a quarter of it but it tasted sour and unappetising so she poured the rest down the kitchen sink and then washed and dried the mug carefully and put it away again in the cupboard, killing time, waiting for she did not know what. And nothing happened.

She roamed the house, anaesthetised into numbness, feeling nothing. She looked at the stags' heads adorning the walls of the hall without either loathing or delight. She wandered guiltily through the rooms like an interloper who simply didn't belong here amongst all the relics of a faded gentility: the billiard room where the old table still sat shrouded in dustsheets, unused for decades. She lifted a corner of the dustsheet and saw that the cloth was pockmarked with moth holes and the slate showed through. She carefully replaced the dustsheet, though that seemed a little pointless now, and roamed through to the gun room which now held no guns, then to the conservatory at the back where the vines were long dead, and she didn't even have the desire to replant them and try to make them grow again. She felt nothing. Nothing for the house, nothing for Glendarroch, nothing for the loch or the hills, nothing except a deep ache of regret for the wrong chances taken and the right chances missed.

She found herself in the vast hall again, from which the staircase rose to split in two directions and disappear to the upper floor, the panelling gleaming darkly and the red carpet soft underfoot. The grandfather clock in the hall ticked sonorously, one tick regularly every second and she opened the door and stood for a while watching the pendulum swing steadily to and fro, counting off the passing moments of their lives.

Where was he? She didn't want to leave the house, but when her wanderings took her back to the kitchen she could see through the window that the outhouse which they used as a garage was still locked, and she felt that if he had taken the car the noise would have woken her, so where had he gone and what was he doing?

And, most importantly, was he coming back?

Eventually she found herself sitting at the bare wooden kitchen table, staring dully out of the window, seeing nothing. Hope and expectation had died. She wasn't hungry, but her eyes seemed to be stinging and she washed her face under the cold water tap at the sink and dried it on the hand towel which hung above the draining board. It didn't make her feel any better.

The house, in spite of its size, seemed to have closed in on her. She sat feeling very small, very much alone, and at that moment even the sight of Sneddon might have been a relief.

At half past eleven she heard the crunch of feet on the gravel outside, and she recognised the step. She rose slowly to her feet, feeling her heart start to pound in her chest.

The back door opened and he came in. She looked at him longingly, but dared not make any move towards him. He seemed pale and there were dark smudges under his eyes, and she knew that he had slept even less than she had.

He closed the door quietly behind him, stood with his hands behind him holding the handle and stared back at her.

She was unaware of any gesture, any expression which might have been a summons but suddenly she was in his arms, and she wasn't sure how she had got there, but they must both have moved towards each other, because they met at a sort of halfway point. His arms were very strong round her, squeezing her to him in a way they hadn't done for a long, long time, and then his mouth was on hers, searching, hungry and desperate. She felt the tears trickling down her face and she thought that she must look an absolute wreck, and when he released her mouth she heard herself say, "I'm sorry, I'm sorry, I'm sorry," over and over again, until he stopped her with another kiss, and she felt herself melting into him in a way which hadn't happened for ages.

An hour and a lifetime later she raised herself on her elbows and looked down at him as he lay beside her in the bed and traced the line from his nose to his mouth with her forefinger. She said nothing and time seemed to hang suspended.

"What you said down there," he said quietly at last.

"Being sorry?"

"Yes. It's me that should be sorry. It wouldn't ever have happened if it hadn't been for me."

"It was just — things."

"Aye. Things. But I'm not going to have you blaming yourself for it, see? Neither you nor this Jimmy Blair."

"Nor yourself either."

"Well, maybe all three of us together were to blame, eh?"

He wanted an answer, so she nodded.

"Yes, all right," she said.

"I'm glad you told me. Can we forget it now?" he asked.

"I think so. I hope so."

"Right."

He kissed her nose and she snuggled back into the crook of his arm, and they lay in a contented silence for quite a long time.

"Sneddon'll be in for his lunch soon," she said.

"Let him."

She was about to protest and then wondered why she should bother about Sneddon anyway. He'd get his own meal as he always did, pass the time of day briefly if either of them was there and then disappear again. One thing was certain — he wouldn't come up here.

"I went to see Mrs Blair this morning," said Harry. She stiffened.

"Oh?" she said, trying to keep her voice non-committal.

"I told her not to blame you for her son leaving. I said it was my fault and I told her why. I thought it was the least I could do."

"What did she say?"

"We got on very well. She's a nice woman."

"Aye, she is."

"And it was her husband who saved me yesterday."

"Him and Eddie."

"Yes. Now, listen, I've had an idea. I want to do something for the lifeboat, right? But I don't just want to write a cheque. That's too easy. I want to do something myself for it. So do you know what I'm going to do?"

"No. What?"

"This'll kill you. And I hope it'll kill Sneddon too. I'm going to do a concert. Here. At Letir-Falloch. In the grounds. For all the locals."

The new idea confused her and she didn't know how to react to it.

"But when . . .?"

"Saturday."

"As soon as that? You couldn't organise it in that time."

"Couldn't I just? Anyway, *I'm* not going to organise it. I'll just be doing it. Sneddon will organise it."

She giggled involuntarily, for the first time seeing a bright flash of humour in the idea.

"He'll love that," she said.

"I know. Can you see it? He's going to have to find a marquee and seats and things. It's a pity I can't land him with the job of finding a P.A. system, but I'll get Bill and Ben up from Glasgow with that lot. Know what? It'll be just like we used to do in the old days. Except for Sneddon. He's going to have a great time."

"Do you need all that — marquees and things?"

"Course I do. It's got to be done properly. Suppose it rains? We'll need a marquee for shelter. Refreshments, too. There's a thought. D'you think we can get Sneddon to make the sandwiches? Maybe not. They'd probably be the pits."

"Harry —"

"Let's go and tackle him about it, eh? That'll spoil his lunch. Come on. Put some clothes on or you'll give him a heart attack, and we don't want that to happen. Not till the concert's over anyway."

He was dressed and out of the room before she had slipped out of bed, and she dressed a great deal more slowly, feeling a great weight of care lifted from her heart. But there was worry there, too. Harry was back to his normal self, he was facing the idea of doing a concert without the fear which such an idea had made him feel since America. Perhaps the thought that he was doing it for a good cause helped, but she was worried that this new-found enthusiasm was based on impracticability and because of that the concert might never take place.

7

Through the drawing room window Sneddon watched the Panda disappear down the drive and felt rage bubbling inside him. He found his hands clenched so tightly that the knuckles showed parchment white and he longed to have someone within reach to hit. Instead he punched the back of an upholstered chair so that the dust flew from it and nearly choked him. Also, unfortunately, there was a wooden strut across the top of the chair, invisible under the upholstery, which caught his fist and jarred his knuckles and he muttered a curse of pain and frustration.

Damn it, who did he think he was, ordering him around like that? All right, to all intents and purposes Shaw was his boss, but that simply meant that he earned the money which paid his wages. Sneddon took his orders from Charlie Davenport and no one else, because it was Charlie who had put him in here and who had told him right at the start that it would be a good thing if the estate didn't exactly make money, but at the same time didn't lose too much either. It was a delicate balance and so far he had managed to draw it to perfection.

And there were little side-lines where he could do a bit of nest-feathering on his own account and which never needed to show in the balance sheet. Although he didn't want to lose that, there were limits to what he could take.

For the first time he had been confronted by his official employer and had been issued specific instructions and, what was worse, the instructions were totally impractical, even if he had been prepared to carry them out.

He had to know where he stood, whether he had to take orders from young Shaw and his woman or whether he stuck by Charlie Davenport.

Sucking his hurt knuckle he made his way to the office and, picking up the telephone receiver, dialled the number of Charlie Davenport's office in Shaftesbury Avenue.

"Davenport and Goldsmith," said the female voice at

the other end of the line.

"Mr Davenport, please," he said.

"Mr Davenport is engaged at the moment can I take a message?" came the mechanically efficient voice at the other end.

"For God's sake, get me Mr Davenport," he snarled. "This is Sneddon at Letir-Falloch."

"One moment please, I'll see if Mr Davenport is available."

The line went dead and he stood waiting impatiently, his temper if anything deteriorating.

"Go ahead please," said the voice.

"Sneddon? How's it going, boy? Our friends arrived safe?"

"Aye, they're here —"

"Fine, fine. How's the weather? Scotch mist all over the place, eh? They got to enjoy themselves, Sneddon, know what I mean? That's what they're there for after all, innit?"

"Oh, they're enjoying themselves all right," said Sneddon. "He nearly got himself drowned yesterday and had to be rescued from the loch by the lifeboat."

"What?" Charlie Davenport's voice was a squawk of dismay. "What you let him go out on the lake alone for, Sneddon?"

"Have you ever tried to stop him?"

"He's all right, is he? No damage nor nothing?"

"No, no damage, but he's grateful to the lifeboat people and the lifeboat's short of money and he's going to set up a concert in the grounds here to raise money for it."

Davenport's voice rose another octave.

"He's what?" he screeched.

"That's what he said. He's just told me to order a marquee and he's off to arrange the refreshments and get the publicity out. And a few other things. And all of it by Saturday."

"*This* Sat'day?"

"This Saturday."

Charlie Davenport swore fluently and loudly and even in his present preoccupied state of mind Sneddon listened with some admiration. Also with some satisfaction at having caused Charlie Davenport a certain amount of distress.

"You got to stop this, Sneddon," said Charlie Davenport as he ran out of things to say and his voice returned to its normal lower pitch.

"Eh?"

"There's not going to be no concert, boy, you understand me?"

"It would take a tank to stop him, the way he's feeling at the moment."

"If it takes a tank, get a tank. There's going to be no concert, my boy, none. Never. Not anyhow. Know what I mean?"

All the negatives didn't help the basic point.

"And how do we stop him?"

"*We* don't stop him, boy. You do. It's up to you. You're the man on the spot. So you stop it. Any way you like. Someone like Vincent doing a gig in a tinpot place like — what's it called — that shanty village near you —?"

"Glendarroch."

"That's it. Glendarrock. You stop it, Sneddon. That's an order."

"How, for God's sake?"

"I don't care how. Just so long as you do it. And listen. No violence, understand me? Harry's not to be hurt. He's a valuable property, Sneddon. To you and me both, boy. Now don't stand there gossiping. Get on with it. Pronto."

The receiver went down at the other end, and Sneddon was left holding his trying to crush it into plastic shards in his hand.

8

Mr MacPherson beamed round the table.

"I am so glad you were all able to get here at such short notice," he said. "I wouldn't have asked you to come except for the fact that I have received some very welcome news, and as there is a certain urgency about the matter I thought it better not to delay things at the outset."

They were looking puzzled and some of them a little put out, he thought, rather relishing the job he was about to perform. Mr Murdoch sat on one side of him looking portentous as usual. It was a face Mr Murdoch inevitably wore at committee meetings, and he was sure it was simply a means of increasing his powers of concentration. Archie Menzies on the other hand, as chairman of the committee, was sitting back looking as though he hadn't a care in the world. Of course, getting away from Glendarroch House in order to attend a meeting was one of Archie's great joys. It saved him from having to do any work. Eddie Ramsay sat opposite him, watching him with interest. Eddie had improved enormously over the last few years. Who would have thought it of Fraser Ramsay's son? It just showed that there was innate goodness in every human being if it only had a chance to get out. Eddie, the ne'er-do-weel, the useless, the discarded, now a respectable member of the lifeboat committee, the man who ran the local ferry and almost always coxed the lifeboat when it was needed. Eddie had had responsibility thrust upon him and had responded splendidly.

Mr MacPherson beamed again.

"We have been worried for some time about the need for maintenance of the lifeboat," he said. "Well, I have to tell you that not an hour ago I had a visit from a young man, known I think to most of you, who has volunteered to help us raise what could be a very large sum indeed."

Eddie Ramsay sat up suddenly.

"Harry Shaw," he said.

"Yes, Eddie. Harry Shaw came to see me with his wife. I understand you rescued him from the loch yesterday."

"That's right, Minister."

"Well, apparently Mr Shaw has been worried about how he could repay you for what you did."

"He could always write a cheque," said Archie. "I wouldn't have thought he'd have much difficulty in finding a pen. Or the money."

"I'm sure that's true," said Mr MacPherson. "He said as much, but he feels that's too easy. He wants to do something personally. So he's had the idea of holding a concert in the grounds of Letir-Falloch for all the local people from Glendarroch and Auchtarne."

"A concert?" said Mr Murdoch.

"Yes. I understand Mr Shaw is a singer, and quite a well-known one amongst the younger members of the population. He has been on the television many times. I hadn't realised what a celebrity we had in our midst."

"This will be a pop concert," said Mr Murdoch.

"I believe so, Mr Murdoch."

Mr Murdoch sniffed in disapproval.

"Maybe you and Mrs Mack would like to do *Madam Will You Walk* again, like you did at our concert here," said Archie. "Just to raise the tone a bit."

Mr Murdoch bridled and Mr MacPherson searched frantically in his mind for some oil to pour on troubled waters, but he was saved the necessity by Eddie.

"That's a great idea," he said. "A concert by Vincent would be a sell out."

Mr Murdoch sniffed again.

"If it were a sell out that would save me from having to go," he said.

"I daresay the style of concert would not be our cup of tea, Mr Murdoch," said Mr MacPherson, "but if it gives pleasure to the young people and if it raises money for the lifeboat and if it appeases Mr Shaw's conscience then it can only be good."

Mr Murdoch wriggled in his chair and murmured something which sounded like "drugs".

"Rubbish," said Eddie who must have heard him more clearly than he had done himself. "It's a great idea, Minister. I think we should accept it."

"I second that," said Archie.

"I'm not sure that you can do that since you're in the chair," said Mr Murdoch.

"Then I shall second it," said Mr MacPherson.

"When is it to be?" asked Eddie.

"Saturday, I understand."

"This Saturday?"

"It's not much notice, I know, but Mr Shaw says he has to leave here by the following Wednesday, so he would like to do it as quickly as possible."

"No wonder he's asking for help," said Eddie. "And he'll need publicity fast."

"Mr Menzies has had experience of designing posters," said Mr MacPherson.

"With the wrong date on them," said Mr Murdoch.

"Not this time, though," said Archie. "This time they'll be real works of art. I've often wanted to design pop concert posters. This is my big chance."

"That is excellent," said Mr MacPherson. "I'm quite sure there will be a great deal for us to do, and I took the liberty of telling Mr Shaw that I thought there would be no trouble in getting people to offer help. This could be the saving of the lifeboat. A chance in a thousand, and we must make the most of it."

And he beamed round the table at them again.

9

Power gave you control over people and controlling people gave you more power. It was a continuing process, thought Sneddon, and he'd taken the first step when he had got this appointment at Letir-Falloch. He had enjoyed the business of choosing his own staff, of giving them orders, of dismissing them when he didn't think they were pulling their weight, of trying his best to get the better of the stuck-up Lady Laird on the next estate. That had given him a taste for power and it had been good.

But now he realised that that power, quickly and easily gained, could be lost just as quickly and just as easily.

His recent confrontations with Harry Shaw and even Sally Shaw, who had once been like a puppet on a string to him, had suddenly wiped the ground from under his feet, and he was left drifting aimlessly, angry, of course, as who wouldn't be, but, what was worse, also humiliated and confused.

He strode away from the house towards the spot where Shaw had said he wanted the concert held just to prove to his own satisfaction how impractical the whole idea was.

"It's a great place, Sneddon," Shaw had said before he and the woman had belted off towards Glendarroch in the car. "Just right. Near enough the house to run the cables from it. Nice country atmosphere. I'll do *I've Gotta Have Trees For You*. Maybe start the whole thing that way. Get it off in the right mood. So you go and have a look at it and see where we can pitch the marquee."

Sneddon had echoed the word "marquee" and Shaw had slapped him on the back in friendliness and enthusiasm.

"Yes. A marquee, of course. Suppose it rains on Saturday? No one'll turn up and the whole thing'll be a frost. Get the biggest marquee you can lay your hands on. There must be someone in Auchtarne who deals with that sort of thing. If not, try Glasgow or Edinburgh. The cost doesn't matter. Just get it here."

His talk had all been of marquees and posters and how to attract everyone for miles around. All that had been bad enough but after Sneddon had called Charlie Davenport, he'd got totally contradictory orders to have the concert stopped.

How the hell was he going to please them both? Whatever he did would incur the wrath of one of them. And both had power to control *him*.

All in all he had the feeling it would be better to keep Charlie Davenport sweet. After all, although Shaw was the one who earned the money it was Charlie Davenport who dealt with it, so he had the greater power.

The patch of bare land which Shaw had said was ideal for the concert lay in a dip just behind the house and there was a fringe of trees and bushes which hid the house from it.

He pushed his way angrily through the bushes and on to the open expanse beyond, and there saw something which made him even angrier than he had been before.

That damned American was there again, down on his hands and knees, crawling all over the ground. The man was like a fly. No matter how many times you brushed it off it still came back for more.

And how on earth had he got here? Sneddon had been in the house all morning and would have noticed anyone passing it to reach this spot, surely.

He shouted and strode towards him, fists clenched, really feeling that this time he would let the man have it, but in any case determined that as the only way to get rid of a fly was to crush it, so he would have to crush this man to get rid of him once and for all. He knew that threatening him with the police was no use. The man wasn't breaking the law. In any case, Sneddon wasn't all that keen on bringing the police into it. In a way this was rapidly becoming a personal vendetta. So all he could do was to put the fear of death into the man. He thought he'd done that already, but evidently not. This time, with the way he was feeling now, he thought he would be able to do it very successfully.

The man rose to his feet as Sneddon advanced on him and stood there waiting quite calmly.

"Listen," said Sneddon as he came up to him, and he grabbed the man by the front of the blue anorak he was wearing. "How many times have I got to tell you to get the hell off this land before it penetrates your thick skull?"

The man regarded him without fear, which was annoying in itself.

"Let go of my jacket, please," he said with such calm authority that Sneddon found himself complying. The man readjusted his lapels.

"Your question is one which only you can answer, sir," he said quietly.

"Then I'm answering it now. This is the last. Understand me? Unless you're out of here in two minutes flat I shall help you out. Physically."

"That, I believe, would be assault."

"Aye. It might be. If you could prove it."

"I find your attitude very difficult to understand, sir, and I can only repeat my request to meet Mr Shaw and have a word with him. Two minutes of his time should be sufficient."

"You'll get none of his time. Not now. Not ever. That's what I'm here for. To save him from the likes of you. Now get!"

"No, sir. I'm afraid not. You see, very soon I shall have the weight of authority behind me."

"Oh, aye? And what authority would that be now?"

"The Government."

"Oh, really? I don't see them standing here."

"No, but you will tomorrow morning. And in view of

that fact you would be well advised to allow me to explain what I am doing here."

There was such certainty as well as such command in his voice that Sneddon made the fatal mistake of pausing and giving him a chance to go on.

"This particular patch of land, sir, which I came across this morning for the first time, is, I believe, a prehistoric site of the most critical importance."

"A prehistoric site?" Sneddon echoed unbelievingly. All this for a load of pansy rubbish like that?

"Yes, sir. In spite of your somewhat crude methods of trying to stop me I have managed to make a brief survey of much of this land. There are several sites of possible interest, but this one is undoubtedly the greatest. You will notice the humps on the ground. Do you see anything significant in them?"

The man swept his hand in a brief arc, embracing the open ground in front of them and Sneddon stared at the area indicated in bafflement.

"They're just molehills. Old molehills grown over," he said.

"I think not. Some of them, perhaps, but not all. Not the important ones." He seized Sneddon by the elbow with unexpected strength and began to propel him round the cleared area, pointing out the spots where almost non-existent little mounds lay half-hidden in the long grass. "See there. And there. And there. Those are not molehills. And do you not see any significance in their distribution?"

Sneddon felt that the initiative was being wrenched away from him and he could only shake his head.

"They form a circle, sir. A definite circle. If we were to strip away the top layers of soil I feel certain we would find the remains of standing stones, perhaps even the stumps of some of them, which would indicate a neolithic stone circle."

"But there aren't any stones —" Sneddon grasped at the only point he had been able to understand so far.

"No, sir. Not like Callanish or Stenness, but the foundations are there sir. Mind you, that in itself is not unusual. Sites of this type are fairly common. No, what excites me, sir, is this. In the centre. Do you notice anything?"

Sneddon stared and became aware that there was a much bigger hump in the ground where the man indicated. It was no higher but seemed to cover a larger area.

"Another molehill," he said.

"Made by a giant mole in that case, sir," said the man with cheerfulness born of excitement and enthusiasm. "No. I'm not sure yet what that is. It could be some central area of the original circle, which would be most unusual, or it could be a more recent overlay of the Bronze Age period. Perhaps a grave. Perhaps a dwelling place. But something which must be investigated and researched thoroughly in the interests of archaeology. Now do you understand something of what I mean?"

Things were stirring at the back of Sneddon's mind. He wasn't sure yet what all this nonsense had to do with the British Cabinet coming here tomorrow, but he had a feeling that somewhere at the end of the tunnel of his ignorance a small light was beginning to glow.

"Maybe I do," he said slowly. "So what happens now?"

"This afternoon, sir, I shall contact the Department of Ancient Monuments in Edinburgh and ask them to send an Inspector here at the earliest opportunity. I shall stress the potential importance of the find, and as my name is not unknown in archaeological circles I feel sure that they will send someone as soon as possible."

"And then?"

"Then the site will be taken over by the Department for thorough investigation. Now, that will happen with or without your co-operation, sir. The owner, of course, will be compensated financially for any loss incurred, but the site will be preserved."

Sneddon stroked his chin thoughtfully.

"And suppose I — suppose the owner refused to allow you access?" he asked.

"I trust you will not hinder such an important operation, sir." The man's voice sounded shocked as though, after his explanation, such an attitude was simply not possible. "This is one of the reasons why I had hoped to speak to Mr Shaw myself."

"I'm not sure that Mr Shaw would allow you to do

this," said Sneddon as the light began to grow in his tunnel. "You see, at the moment he has an eye on this site for a pop concert on Saturday. I'm here to survey it for a marquee and we'll have to dig holes for fence posts for crowd control and —"

The man was looking at him in growing horror.

"A pop concert? Thousands of feet trampling all over the site? Excavations for fence posts —?"

Sneddon nodded.

"Tent pegs too," he said.

"Good Lord, sir! This cannot be allowed!"

Sneddon smiled at him, and in his anxiety the man didn't even seem to find that strange.

"How would you stop it then?"

"The Department of Ancient Monuments —"

"Look, Mister, this Department of Ancient Monuments doesn't sound as if it could move fast enough to prevent something which is going to happen this Saturday, now, does it?"

The man thought for a few moments.

"Then a direct application to the Secretary of State for Scotland would ensure that nothing was allowed to take place here without prior approval," he said.

"And that approval might take a wee while to get, eh?"

"It would indeed."

Sneddon nodded, satisfied.

"That's what I wanted to hear," he said. "In other words, you go to the Secretary of State and tell him the story and he says right, no concert, folks, not until we have a proper look at the place, right?"

"Exactly."

It was like a miracle, he thought. Here he'd been frantically looking for some way of stopping the concert and he was suddenly being offered the assistance of the Secretary of State for Scotland by the man he'd been trying to kick off the estate for the best part of a week.

"Well, now, perhaps you'd like to tell me a little bit more about this site, and then I'll take you to my office and you can ring your Ancient Monuments from there."

The man looked at him in amazement.

"You have changed your tune, sir, if I may say so," he said.

"Let's say that you've convinced me that what you're
doing is very important," said Sneddon smoothly and in
his turn he began to guide the man back towards the
house. "I wonder now, do you happen to know the
Secretary of State's telephone number offhand?"

Chapter Four

1

The sky had cleared again by the Monday and the sun was already warm when Eddie and Sheila made their way down from the cottage to the jetty to take the ferry over to Auchtarne.

"Sure you want to come?" he asked her.

"Yes, of course. There are lots of things I must get in Auchtarne. And when I get back there'll be plenty to do before Saturday."

"It looks like being a quiet crossing this way, anyway," he said as they reached the jetty and found the ferry floating motionless at its moorings and no one in sight anywhere around.

"Everyone's too busy to bother about going to Auchtarne today," she said.

"Aye. You wouldn't rather go up to Letir-Falloch and see if the Shaws want any help?"

She shook her head.

"No. It's heavy work to start with and there'll be enough people up there for that. And I'm not going up there with that Sneddon around the place. He can't keep his hands to himself."

"If he laid a finger on you I'd pulverise him."

"Would you?"

"Sure I would."

"Maybe you would. Well, I'm not going to give you the chance of being up for assault and battery. That's why I'm coming to Auchtarne with you."

Eddie looked at his watch. It was a minute past eight and still no one in sight.

"Well, this is always the quiet run when the school's on holiday," he said. "And none of the tourists will be out of their beds yet."

"We could have stayed in ours and not bothered to go."

"There'll be plenty coming over from Auchtarne on the return run."

He glanced at his watch again.

"Right. Let's go," he said. "We can be on our own for once."

He jumped on board, removed the tarpaulin cover from the engine casing and packed it in the locker, then pressed the starter. The engine fired after a couple of turns and Sheila went and stood by the mooring lines.

"I'm glad we've been asked to help set up the concert," he said.

"I'm sure everyone in the village feels the same," she said as she released the bow line.

"Makes you feel you're doing something for the lifeboat yourself."

"I'm just glad to have the chance to be working for Vincent," she said.

"Oh, aye. Stars in your eyes, are there?"

"Maybe a wee bit."

"Mphm. His hands would be different from Sneddon's, eh?"

"It's different. He's got a wife to keep him in order and Sneddon hasn't."

He grinned at her.

"Okay, cast off," he said and she coiled the line and put it on the bow thwart and then went to the stern.

"It's not much notice, though, is it?" she asked.

"What, the concert on Saturday? No, it isn't. Still, the news'll never have a chance to go stale."

She coiled the stern line and stepped aboard with it. He moved the lever forward and the ferry slid gently away from the jetty and out into the loch.

It was calm again and the sun was lifting over the eastern hills, glimmering on the water like a thousand jewels which were never still. The air was as clear as he had ever seen it, and behind them the houses of Glendarroch and the hills beyond were pin sharp in the sunlight.

She came and stood beside him and he put an arm round her as he steered with his other hand.

"I wonder if Jimmy misses all this?" he said after a long silence.

"He must do," she said. "Who wouldn't?"

"Aye. Who wouldn't? And I sometimes wonder if he misses Sally Shaw."

"I wonder if *she* misses *him*. I've got a feeling that she doesn't any more."

"Think not?"

"Well — not as much as she did."

"Folk are fickle," he said after a minute.

"So they are now."

He felt her arm go round him as though to deny her agreement and he bent and kissed her gently as the ferry surged on towards Auchtarne.

2

"What do you think Lorna?" asked Archie, and she looked up from her typewriter at the sheet of drawing paper he held under her nose.

"It's very nice, Archie," she said. "What is it?"

"It's a poster for the concert," said Archie, as though talking to an idiot. "Don't you recognise a guitar when you see one?"

Lorna looked at it critically.

"That's not a guitar, Archie," she said. "That's a violin."

Archie snorted.

"Where's your musical knowledge?" he asked. "A violin hasn't got six strings."

"No," said Lorna, "but a guitar hasn't got a bridge either."

Archie looked carefully at the drawing for a minute.

"Well, that's not exactly a bridge," he said at last.

"Really? What is it then?"

"A smudge. I'll fill it in later."

"Oh, I see. Well, otherwise, it's very good, Archie. Go to the top of the class."

Fiona came into the office from the hall and headed for her own door.

"Are those the leaflets, Lorna?" she asked.

"Yes. Just finishing the fair copy," said Lorna, "then it's straight into the photocopier."

"Good."

She stopped to look at Archie's poster which he was holding in a conspicuous manner for her to see.

"That looks good, Archie," she said. "Got the date right this time?"

"I wish I had a pound for every time someone's asked me that," Archie muttered, turning the poster to look at it. "Yes," he said. "Saturday 31st. It's down there in black and white."

"Saturday's the 29th, Archie," said Fiona.

"It isn't, is it?" said Archie in a tone of voice which deceived neither of them. They waited patiently for the denouement. He held the poster out to them with a flourish. "Ta-ra!" he said. "Saturday 29th, just as the calendar says."

Fiona shook her head in pity and examined the poster critically.

"It's very good, Archie, but why has the guitar got a bridge?" she asked.

He sighed and glanced at Lorna.

"It's just a wee mistake I made. I'm going to blot it out with a deft stroke of the pen and then it's into the photocopier with it."

"Lorna, I'm worried about the outlying places getting word of the concert. With the school holidays on just now it's difficult to contact folk."

"Maybe we could get Donnie to spread some of the leaflets around with the post bus."

"That's a good thought. I'll get on to the post office at Auchtarne."

"I'm not sure that I'd do that, Fiona. If you make it official you'll have to pay. Have a word with Donnie when he gets here this morning. He'll probably do it for a couple of tickets for his kids."

"Good idea. Well, if this concert's not a roaring success it certainly won't be for want of trying," said Fiona cheerfully and went into her office.

Archie surveyed the poster gloomily.

"Know what?" he said, licking a finger and experimentally rubbing the poster with it. "I've learnt something today."

"What's that, Archie?"

"You should cross out your bridges before some clever Dick notices them," he said.

3

"There is one thing certain, Minister. Not one of these chairs is leaving this hall," said Mrs Mack, standing in front of a pile of them as though determined to defend them with her life against all-comers.

"But Mrs Mack, the chairs will be needed inside the marquee for the audience," said Mr MacPherson. "If we are to get the size of audience we hope for we shall need every available chair we can find, and these ones would make an enormous difference."

"Over my dead body, Mr MacPherson," said Mrs Mack. "I know exactly what will happen. Half of them will get smashed up, which is what usually happens at these affairs, and those that do get returned will be covered in bubble-gum and worse. I am not going to have the job of cleaning them after they have been used in that fashion by young thugs."

"I hardly think the audience will consist of young thugs," said Mr MacPherson.

"Mr Murdoch will bear me out," said Mrs Mack, and Mr Murdoch looked a little uncomfortable at being thus caught between two stools.

"Well," he said, "there is certainly something in what you say, Mrs Mack, but on the other hand the lifeboat does need the money which this concert will un- doubtedly raise."

"Blood money, Mr Murdoch. Money earned in this unsavoury manner can bring no good to the lifeboat."

"I don't quite understand how the lifeboat will be affected by where the money comes from, so long as it comes," said Mr MacPherson.

Mrs Mack glared at him pityingly.

"Mr MacPherson, you know as well as I do what these pope concerts are."

Mr MacPherson felt that was probably very true. He knew absolutely nothing about pop concerts and he suspected that, if anything, Mrs Mack knew even less.

"I have seen them on the television," said Mrs Mack. "Noise and sweat and heaving bodies and — and unspeakable things of that kind."

"I have myself seen pop concerts on the television," said Mr MacPherson mildly, "and while I have to confess they do very little for me, I have seen more suggestive movement and closeness such as you imply in ordinary ballroom dancing. It appears that the gyrations at these events never actually involve physical contact at all. Each person — what is the phrase? — does his or her own thing."

"No chairs, Minister. They can find their seating elsewhere."

Mr MacPherson sighed deeply.

"Very well," he said. "If that is your decision, Mrs Mack, I have to accept it. I would simply ask that over the next twenty-four hours or so you will examine your conscience very carefully indeed."

Mrs Mack drew herself up as though her conscience had already been examined and had not been found wanting, and the minister left the hall feeling that on this particular issue, as on so many others, he had come off second best.

4

Isabel fixed the poster to the glass front of the post office counter and stood back to look at it. Archie had done a good job, she thought, though there seemed to be a slight fuzziness at one point in the background picture of a guitar. But the lettering stood out boldly, which was the main thing.

! CONCERT !
AT LETIR-FALLOCH HOUSE
SATURDAY 29TH JULY AT 7.30 P.M.
FEATURING THE ONE AND ONLY
!!! VINCENT !!!
IN AID OF THE LOCH DARROCH LIFEBOAT
MAINTENANCE FUND
FIRST COME FIRST SERVED!
REFRESHMENTS FREE!
£1 IF YOU LOVE THE LIFEBOAT + £1 IF YOU LOVE
VINCENT!

IF YOU LOVE BOTH THE SKY'S THE LIMIT!!!!

Yes, it really looked very good, though she thought that perhaps Archie had been a little heavy-handed with the exclamation marks, and she nodded in approval.

The door opened and she turned.

She wasn't quite sure how to react. She had told Harry Shaw that she didn't blame Sally for what had happened between her and Jimmy, but saying it was easy. It was very difficult to mean it. And now, far too soon, before she had had time to adjust to the idea, Sally Shaw stood in front of her with Harry beside her.

"Hallo, Mrs Blair," said Sally.

Isabel suddenly realised that Sally was as nervous and embarrassed as she was herself, and she remembered what Harry had said on Saturday.

"Hallo, Sally," she said, and as far as she could remember it was the first time she had called her by her first name.

There was a long and awkward silence.

"Harry said I shouldn't come," she said, "but I wanted to — to —"

"Get it over with," said Isabel with a slightly strained smile.

Sally's answering smile was equally strained.

"Well — something like that," she said.

"We've been around talking to everyone else in Glendarroch that we could find. Asking them to help with the concert," said Harry. "Sally thought it wouldn't be a good idea if you heard about it and we hadn't been in here too."

Isabel smiled and this time it felt less strained.

"I'd say that was good thinking," she said. "And I've certainly heard of it. Archie Menzies was in not ten minutes ago."

She indicated the poster and Harry Shaw, after a brief glance at Sally, squeezed her hand and went to have a look at it, leaving the two of them together.

"I'm sorry, Mrs Blair," said Sally after a moment, and her voice sounded a little muffled. When Isabel looked more closely she saw that the girl was close to tears.

"Och, don't," she said, not quite sure whether she was

telling her not to be sorry, or telling her not to cry, because if she did the latter Isabel felt she would probably join her.

"But I am. What a mess. I wish it had never happened."

"There's no point in wishing that," said Isabel. "It has, and there's nothing we can do about it, except get on with the business of living. You've got a lot of that to do yet, so just you do it. The pair of you."

Sally hesitated for a moment and then stepped forward and kissed her on the cheek.

"You're a terribly good person," she said.

"Havers," said Isabel. "If you knew me better you wouldn't say that. Ask Brian or Jimmy —"

She stopped, wishing she could bite her tongue off, and the name echoed into silence while they seemed frozen. She could almost feel the effort Sally made to restore normality to the situation.

"Do you hear from him?" she asked.

Isabel nodded.

"Every now and again. He's in Glasgow. He seems well. And happy. I think. Reading between the lines. He was never much of a letter writer, though, so it's difficult to tell."

Sally opened her mouth as though she were going to ask something else, and then thought better of it.

"I'm glad," she said. "I think we ought to go now."

She turned to Harry in a sort of mute appeal and he came to her immediately.

Isabel nodded.

"You'll come to the concert, Mrs Blair?" said Harry.

Isabel smiled at them both, and this time there was no strain in it at all.

"Try to keep me away," she said.

5

"Well," said Alice as she watched the Panda disappearing down the track from the cottage, "I never thought I'd live to see the day that Vincent sat right here in our own living room."

"Just like having the Queen to tea, isn't it?" agreed

Bob.

"Och, you!" she said. "You know what I mean. Fame has come to Glendarroch."

"He seems a nice lad."

"Yes. We'll have to go to the concert."

"I suppose we will."

"Don't you want to go?"

"Aye. For the sake of the lifeboat, anyway. Though I can't help feeling we'll look terribly old alongside most of the audience. But what do we do with young Donald?"

"Mrs Lachlan'll look after him."

"You don't think Mrs Lachlan mightn't want to go to the concert too?"

Alice stared at him, wondering if he were joking or not.

"Do you think she might?"

"No. But I've got the feeling she might think she *ought*. So asking her to look after Donald might be a blessing in disguise to her."

Alice smiled at him.

"Is that what you call lateral thinking?" she asked.

"I don't call it lateral thinking because I don't even know what it is."

"So for the next few days you'll be at Letir-Falloch doing some work for a change."

"For a change? I like that! Getting this concert organised will be a doddle compared to my normal heavy workload."

"Oh, aye. I wonder what I could make for the refreshments? Maybe some scones and rock cakes?"

"Anything. If this audience is like most audiences they'll probably go through the refreshments like a flock of gannets."

"I'll get down to that tomorrow. The trouble is I won't have all that much time."

"Why not?"

"Well, I want to slip up to Letir-Falloch sometime and see that you've taken your place on the chain-gang."

"I always knew there was a vindictive side to your nature."

"Besides — I wouldn't mind seeing a bit more of Harry Shaw."

"That lad's gone to your head."

"Aye, he has, hasn't he?" she agreed, and she ducked as he threw a cushion at her.

6

"You'll be going to this concert, of course," said Grace.

"I will not," said Dougal as he settled back in his chair and lit his after-lunch pipe.

"It would do you good. See how the other half lives."

"I don't want to see how the other half lives. I've seen enough of it to know I don't like it."

"You haven't seen anything of it at all."

"Well, I've heard enough."

"You want to support the lifeboat, don't you?"

"Aye, I do."

"Well, then."

"But I'm not paying a pound just to have my ears ruined by a man roaring into a microphone."

"Huh!"

"Anyway," he said casually as he opened up last week's copy of *The Crofter and Farmer*, "I don't think this concert's going to happen."

"Of course it's going to happen! Everybody's working for it. Except you."

"Aye, aye."

There was something infuriatingly certain in his attitude which made her look at him more closely.

"Come on," she said. "What is it?"

"What's what?"

"What have you been hearing that no one else has?"

He folded *The Crofter and Farmer* and laid it down on the floor beside his chair.

"Well, if you must know, on my way in to Auchtarne this morning I nearly gave that man MacAulay a dunt as he was coming out of the gates of Letir-Falloch."

"Walking?"

"No. In his car. So I stopped to pass the time of day."

"And to find out why he was using the main gate and not creeping round the hills avoiding the man Sneddon."

"That too."

"And?"

"He told me Sneddon's changed his tune. And he told me he's found that stone circle of his and that Sneddon's helping him with it."

"And he believes Sneddon?"

"Aye. What's more, his stone circle's on the very ground that the concert's to be done on, and MacAulay's getting some Ministry man to put a stop to it so that his circle doesn't get spoilt. What do you think of that now?"

"And Sneddon's helping him?"

"Aye."

"Why?"

"Well, now, I'm not quite sure about that, but MacAulay seems convinced that Sneddon's on his side, and that Sneddon doesn't want the concert to happen. Of course MacAulay doesn't want the concert to happen either, not on his circle, so if Sneddon's against it too you can be pretty sure that the concert won't happen."

"But that's awful!"

"What's awful about it?"

"Everybody working away like beavers for the concert so that they can raise some money for the lifeboat, and if what you say is true, there isn't going to be a concert."

"Aye, well, I'm certainly not paying out a pound for something that's not going to happen, Mother."

And he picked up the paper again as though that were the end of the matter.

7

The morning was as bright as the previous one, and already there was heat in the sun. When it climbed higher and the shadows were short it would be very hot here.

Brian sat on a tree stump at the edge of the clearing where the marquee was to be raised and watched Eddie ranging backwards and forwards in front of him.

"Where is it?" he asked.

"Relax, Eddie. It'll be here," said Brian.

"Look, this is Wednesday. There's a whole heap to be done before Saturday. The marquee itself, the fencing to keep out the ones who haven't paid, besides all the technical stuff which I don't understand."

"Harry Shaw's looking after that himself. That's why he isn't here. He's organising a whole bouroch of electricians in Auchtarne to come and give him a hand tomorrow and Friday once the marquee's up."

"I know, but I want to do something now. If we don't get started soon I'll have to go for the next ferry run and it'll be at least three hours before I can get back."

"I said relax. There are a few other able-bodied men around. It takes time to organise a marquee, you know. They don't grow on trees. And we'll not have everything fixed by the time you get back from the next run."

"If I'd been him I'd have risked it and just held the concert in the open air. Save all this bother."

Brian looked at the sky.

"He'd be taking a chance," he said. "I don't know if the weather's going to hold, and if it breaks it may break for a few days."

"Pessimist."

"Well, there's one thing about being a pessimist. It's always a pleasant surprise when things don't turn out as badly as you think they will."

"Ha, ha," said Eddie morosely.

Bob and Dougal strolled past with a nod of greeting, and further away across the clearing Brian could see Archie and Mr Murdoch talking together, probably totting up the amount of money the lifeboat fund might expect to benefit by at the end of the week. There was an air of expectancy around. Not, thought Brian, that any of those here were madly keen on a pop concert for its own sake, but they were all very keen on what a pop concert might do for the lifeboat.

The sound of a labouring engine came to them across the stillness of the day and Brian rose to his feet.

"This sounds like it now," he said.

A few moments later a heavy lorry came lurching and groaning round the side of the house, a high tarpaulin-covered load on its back, and headed across the rough ground towards the clearing.

"That's it," said Brian. "Well, you can give us five minutes of your valuable time before you have to leave the rest of us to sweat it out here while you go and enjoy yourself on the ferry."

Eddie grinned at him, relieved that at last there was something to do.

The lorry stopped at the edge of the clearing and they gathered round it. Two men got out of the cab and came round to the rear and began to unleash the ropes holding down the load.

As they did so a car approached from the same direction as the lorry and came to a halt beside them. It was almost as though the car must have been following it.

Brian glanced into it and saw the tall, rangy figure of the American, MacAulay, in the driver's seat and sitting beside him was Sneddon. There was someone else in the back but he couldn't make him out.

Sneddon got out of the car.

"Hold it," he said, and the men unleashing the ropes stopped and turned to him. Sneddon looked round and Brian could swear there was satisfaction in that dark and brooding face. "Sorry, folks," said Sneddon, but he didn't sound very sorry. "The deal's off."

"What do you mean the deal's off?" asked Brian.

"Just what I say," said Sneddon. "Can't make it much clearer, can I? Here's the man who can tell you why."

He pointed to MacAulay who had just unwound himself from inside the car and Brian listened as MacAulay went into a long explanation about this being a very important prehistoric site of some kind and that he had been in touch with the Secretary of State and the Department of Ancient Monuments in Edinburgh to have it preserved for proper investigation. Eventually MacAulay's voice stopped and there was silence for a while.

"You mean — we can't use the site?" asked Eddie.

"I'm afraid not, sir," said MacAulay. "I do most sincerely hope this will not cause you any embarrassment, but the site is too important to allow access to it for the sort of purpose I believe you had in mind."

"Now, wait a minute," said Brian. "This land belongs to Harry Shaw, right?"

"Quite correct, sir."

"And Harry Shaw has given us permission to hold the concert here. In fact, he started the whole idea."

"Yes, sir, but that was before we knew about the value of the site. Might I suggest that there must be other sites close to the house where you could hold your concert?"

Eddie shook his head.

"Any further away and there's problems about cable leads," he said. "That's why it had to be so close to the house. Besides, you can't expect people to come here and then walk across acres of soggy fields to get to the thing—"

Brian glanced at Sneddon, because there was something odd going on and anything odd, he felt, could only originate with this man. He was looking — what was it? — smug. That was it. As though he were a cat who had got at the cream, and furthermore a cat who knew that no one else knew he'd got at it. Now, why would that be? he wondered . . .

But he turned back to listen to MacAulay who was still talking.

". . . to Mr Gillies here who is from the Department. He and I are now going to have a thorough look at the site. The final decision whether to recommend to the Department that the site is taken over will rest with him."

Brian looked at the third man who had now climbed out of the car. He was small and sandy-haired with rimless glasses and he stood blinking apologetically in the sunlight and nodding as though in greeting to those who were gathered around him.

Brian found his mind beginning to work again after the first shock of hearing that the site might not be available. There was Sneddon's smugness, there was the arrival of a man from Edinburgh so opportunely, there was what he knew of MacAulay as a decent sort of character . . . And things began to fall into place.

"Mr Gillies?" he said and the little man turned to him and smiled.

"Yes," he said.

"Who got in touch with you?" asked Brian, glancing at Sneddon.

"Mr MacAulay, sir. In person."

"By telephone, I suppose?"

"Yes, sir. You can imagine my surprise, suddenly having to come all the way up here. It is a pleasant change, I have to admit, to get out of the office at this time of year —"

"When was this?" asked Brian, and as he said it Sneddon suddenly stirred into action and another piece of the jigsaw fell into place in Brian's mind.

"Look, let's clear the site, shall we?" he said loudly, "and let Mr MacAulay and Mr Gillies get to work."

"Just a minute," said Brian. "I haven't got an answer to my question yet."

"I rang the Department on Monday afternoon," said Mr MacAulay.

"After you'd spoken to Mr Sneddon, of course," said Brian.

"Now look here —" said Sneddon, but MacAulay overrode him.

"Naturally," he said. "Mr Sneddon was extremely co-operative. I was most agreeably surprised."

"Why was that?" asked Brian.

MacAulay looked slightly embarrassed and Sneddon stepped up to Brian threateningly.

"Would you like to get yourself off Letir-Falloch land right now?" he demanded. "Standing around here as if you were the Lord God Almighty asking questions where you've no right —"

"All right," said Brian. "Let me ask you —" he thrust a finger into Sneddon's chest and made him retreat a step or two "— one question. You knew about not being able to use the land on Monday, right? So you had a lot of Monday and all of yesterday and right up until this moment to tell us that the concert was off and that we could all go home. But you didn't do it. What I want to know is why didn't you tell us?"

There was a murmur and the others moved in to hear what answer Sneddon had to that, but the movement must have looked threatening to him.

"I don't have to answer questions from the likes of you," he blustered.

"Well, then, answer this one," said Eddie suddenly. "Does Harry Shaw know that the concert isn't going to take place?"

Sneddon stuttered for a moment.

"Keep your dirty nose out of other people's business, ferry boy —" he said.

"But I think it is our business," said Eddie. "Mr Shaw's giving this concert to help the lifeboat. I'd have thought he'd be the first to know if it was being cancelled. Why doesn't he? Know what? I think we ought to see him."

"He isn't here."

"We'll wait," said Brian. He looked at the lorry with the tarpaulin still in place on the back. "We haven't got much else to do now."

"I'm extremely sorry if this has caused you problems," said MacAulay, his voice puzzled.

"Not your fault, Mr MacAulay," said Brian. "I think we can see what's happened. But we might as well hang on and see Mr Shaw. Who knows, we might get some questions answered while we wait."

8

Harry slammed the inner front door shut so hard that the glass panel nearly shattered, and stood just inside the hall, trembling with rage.

Sneddon. Damn Sneddon. He'd ruined his idea for the concert, the concert which would have helped to salve his conscience and done something for the local community which he and Sally had between them managed to upset so much. And now this creep had come between him and his aims.

Well, Sneddon would have to sort it out with the locals, and Harry had just told him to do so, leaving him outside the house on the gravel surrounded by angry men who were demanding explanations. Harry had told them that he knew nothing about the cancellation, that the first he had heard of it was on his return from Auchtarne where he had actually been contracting electricians and the chap who ran the local discos to come and rig the lighting. He'd already been on to Bill and Ben in Glasgow and fixed for them to bring the P.A. system up here on the Saturday morning.

Now what?

One thing he was determined about was that Sneddon wasn't going to win this. He had no idea yet why Sneddon had done it, but he would find out all in good time and he'd make the man sweat for it. But meanwhile, the concert had to go ahead, and this time he'd have to have everything tied up completely before Sneddon became aware of it.

He went to Sneddon's office, locked the door behind him, angrily swept papers from the desk to the floor and picked up the telephone directory. He flicked through the pages, found the number he wanted and dialled it.

"District Council, which department, please?" asked a voice at the other end.

"Listen, get me someone who deals with letting the Town Hall," he said.

"One moment, please."

He sat in Sneddon's chair, drumming the fingers of one hand on the desk, waiting.

A minute later he was talking to a disembodied male voice which announced itself as Mr-Petrie-can-I-help-you, and he asked to book the Auchtarne Town Hall for Saturday night.

"I don't know if we can do that," said Mr Petrie. "Hold on a moment." There was the sound of pages being turned and then Mr Petrie spoke again. "Hallo. I'm afraid that's not possible. There's a cookery demonstration organised by the Women's Rural Institute that night."

Harry thought rapidly.

"How about Friday?" he asked.

"This Friday?"

"Aye."

"The day after tomorrow?"

Harry repressed a desire to say that as this was Wednesday it would be quite usual for the day after tomorrow to be Friday, and simply said, "Aye" again.

More pages flicked.

"Yes, sir, you could have the Town Hall on Friday."

Harry breathed a sigh of relief. It was even shorter notice than previously, it would mean altering all the prepared publicity, but it would be in the centre of population and in many ways it was a better venue than

Letir-Falloch.

"I'll come and fix the details," he said.

"That would be quite convenient, sir," said Mr Petrie. "What is the name, please?"

"Harry Shaw."

There was a pause at the other end while Mr Petrie took it in.

"Mr Harry Shaw of Letir-Falloch?" he asked.

"Aye."

"*Vincent*?"

"Aye."

"Oh, my goodness, Mr Shaw. What a privilege to speak to you! My two daughters have all your records. It would be a great pleasure to welcome you here, sir."

"I'll be there in half an hour," said Harry, and he slammed down the receiver and hurried out of the office.

Outside Sneddon was still surrounded by the local people, still trying to explain away his action. Harry would have liked to stay to hear the explanation himself. That was something he was still waiting for. But there were other more pressing things at the moment. He jumped into the Panda, turned the starter and roared off down the drive at top speed.

9

Sally heard the front door slam shut and she sat at the kitchen table, chin in her hands, thinking mixed feelings about what had happened.

She didn't like this enthusiasm for the concert. She could understand his reasons for wanting to do it, but she was afraid that if his urge to get back to this sort of thing became too strong he would be tempted to return to the big-time far too soon for his own health.

America had been a terrible experience. Of course, she had started off on the wrong foot and her opinion was biased for several different reasons. Leaving Jimmy was the start of it, and she had flown the Atlantic feeling as though she had left most of herself behind. But when they had taken her into that sterile hospital room and she had seen the pale, helpless face lying on the pillow, she had felt her heart go out to him in a way it hadn't done before. Since then she had nursed him gently back to health and sanity, brought him home to the London flat, and while she had not been keen to return to Letir-Falloch she had done so because when he suggested it she was sure that it would do him good.

Now, however, it looked as if they might be going back to square one. She knew that Charlie Davenport was beavering away in the background, anxious to get Harry back as soon as he could, and she wanted to postpone that day for as long as possible. At least now her main reasons for not wanting to come here had gone. She had made the confession which she had known she would have to make sooner or later. It had cleansed her and it hadn't been nearly as bad as she had thought it might be, and Harry had been very good, very generous and understanding about it all.

But what about this concert? First the announcement of it, then the relief of the cancellation because the site would not be available and then his immediate booking of the Town Hall in Auchtarne. And Charlie Davenport wouldn't like that, either. It was all becoming too complicated.

The front door bell rang and she went to answer it. Sneddon and the crowd had dispersed. She didn't know where to and she didn't much care either.

On the doorstep stood a single solitary figure. It was the American, MacAulay.

"Mrs Shaw?" he said and she nodded. "I feel, ma'am, I owe you an explanation for what happened today at the site you wanted for your concert."

"My husband's told me about it," she said. "You needn't worry, Mr MacAulay. It wasn't your fault."

"But I feel mighty bad about it all the same. I have an idea that your man of business may not have told you the whole story. And in case he hasn't I wanted to set the record straight and also to say I was sorry it all worked out this way."

She caught his eye straying past her to survey the interior of the house and she suddenly remembered the rumour she had heard — that this man was a member of the family which had originally owned Letir-Falloch, and so far as she knew he had never seen inside it.

"Would you like to come in?" she asked. "I could give you a cup of coffee. And if you'd like to look round you'd be very welcome."

She saw that she had said the right thing. His face broke into a beaming smile of gratitude.

"I would certainly appreciate the opportunity, ma'am," he said.

"Come in, then."

She had never done a conducted tour of the house before and she quite enjoyed it. As they went slowly through the rooms he told her of his connection with the previous owners and she told him how Harry had bought the place as a tax-loss and she found him surprisingly easy to talk to. She sensed the wonder in him as they moved from room to room and he touched things and examined them gently and almost lovingly, his eyes sometimes absent, face abstracted, and as they left the upstairs rooms and stood at the head of the flight leading into the hall, he paused and looked round.

"It's surprising how wrong imagination can be, isn't it?" he said. "It's not really how I imagined it at all. But now I know. And I can carry the true picture with me for the rest of my life. I can't tell you how glad I am to have seen it."

"You wouldn't like to come back and live here?" she asked.

He looked at her in surprise.

"You're not thinking of selling it, are you?" he asked.

"I don't know what's in Harry's mind these days," she said.

He thought for a while and then shook his head.

"I've seen it now and that's enough," he said. "It's been a wonderful experience just to see what I have heard so much about. But my curiosity is satisfied and I've also found something to set my mind at rest. I don't want to live here either. It's too big."

She nodded agreement.

"Far too big for a private person," she said.

"This sort of place has had its day. Maybe they were good days for those who were able to enjoy them, but it's an anachronism now."

She began to lead the way down the stairs and through the green baize door to the kitchen where she put the kettle on the cooker.

She invited him to sit down at the kitchen table and he did so.

"Your husband is out?" he asked.

"He's tying up the booking of the Town Hall."

"I should appreciate the chance of meeting him."

"I'm sure he'd like to meet you too," she said. "Are you still working at the site?"

He nodded.

"I've left Mr Gillies there," he said. "I must not be too long."

"When Harry comes back I'll tell him where you are. He'll probably come and have a word with you. You tell him what Sneddon said to you and make sure that he knows what's going on. I'm pretty sure he'll be glad if you go ahead."

"You are very kind," he said.

She poured the coffee and they sat talking at the kitchen table as though they had known each other for years.

Ten minutes later she watched him from the morning room window as he left the house and crossed the forecourt on his way back to his site. Before he turned the corner she saw him stop and look back at the house for a moment. Then he nodded briefly to himself as though finally ridding himself of any illusions about the romance of the place and disappeared round the corner.

10

Sneddon slipped into the telephone box at the crossroads feeling like a felon. It was probably unnecessary to come down here to make the call, but the last thing he wanted was to be overheard in the house by either Shaw or his woman, and he had had difficulty enough in getting away from that rabble of yokels. He dialled the operator and asked for a personal reversed charges call to Charlie Davenport at his Shaftesbury Avenue number.

He waited while the connection was made, looking out

at the banks of grass on either side of the road. They were dappled with summer flowers, and he felt none of their brightness and vitality.

Shaw had taken great delight in leaving him to explain matters to the local yokels and he had done it to the best of his ability, hating every minute of it, being unaccustomed to having to explain his actions to anybody, be apologetic, let alone to these people who had been at loggerheads with him since he had arrived at Letir-Falloch. They had eventually gone away, contemptuous and totally dissatisfied.

He'd deliberately allowed Shaw to go ahead and arrange the concert, knowing himself that it wouldn't take place and that once the man from the Department got here it would be inevitably stopped. He had taken great delight in hiring the biggest marquee he could lay his hands on from a firm in Edinburgh, even agreeing to pay over the odds for it because of the shortness of notice, because Shaw would be footing the bill and the thing wasn't going to be used anyway. He hadn't said anything about the cancellation because by withholding the information he would make it much more difficult for Shaw to reorganise things and do the concert somewhere else, so that he felt he had fulfilled Charlie Davenport's instructions very satisfactorily without involving himself in hassle. But that creep Brian Blair had seen the one weak point in it — the delay in letting anyone know. And of course Shaw himself had wasted no time in rearranging the venue.

"Sneddon? What's the trouble?"

Charlie Davenport's voice broke in on his reverie and he brought himself back to the problem in hand.

"I stopped the Letir-Falloch concert," he said.

"Good man. You done what you were told, then. You haven't rung just to tell me that, though, have you?"

"He's rearranged it."

He waited while Charlie Davenport repeated the swearing performance which had taken place last time they had spoken.

"What's he fixed now?" he asked at last.

"Auchtarne Town Hall, Friday night, seven thirty," said Sneddon.

Charlie Davenport was silent at the other end for so long Sneddon wondered if he'd had a heart attack.

"You still there?" he asked at last.

"Course I'm still here!" snapped Charlie Davenport. "I'm thinking, that's all. This isn't very good, Sneddon, know what I mean?"

"I guess it isn't."

"You guess! I bloody well *know*. All right. Look. Leave it. I'll have to handle this myself. Can't trust nobody to do nothing, that's the trouble these days," he added in an undertone which Sneddon felt was really addressed directly to him so he decided not to comment on it. "I'll be up Friday."

"Friday? That's leaving it a bit late, isn't it?"

"Can't help that, boy. I got to be in Stuttgart tomorrow. Can't get out of that, not anyhow. I'll be there Friday morning."

"Okay, but it doesn't leave much time."

"Stop panicking. I've got things to organise this end, see? Plenty things. It's all right. We'll stop it yet. Good God, here's me in Stuttgart tying up the biggest thing he's done since America, and he's sitting there doing a bloody country gig in the Ocktarn Town Hall. The boy needs his head examined."

"What do you want me to do?"

"Just sit on your fanny, boy, and do nothing, see? Then nothing can't go wrong. Leaving it till Friday might make things easier in the long run. Let him go on. Let him plan it, organise it, prepare for it. All that jazz. It won't matter in the long run, know what I mean? See you Friday, boy. Cheers."

The receiver went down and Sneddon hung up himself, wondering what the next couple of days were going to bring, and wishing somehow that they were already well and truly over.

11

The shadows were lengthening over the clearing as the sun sank, and in the west there was a haziness which betokened breaking weather rather than heat. But the

day was still windless and warm and MacAulay sat back
on his haunches and laid his trowel carefully on the
ground beside him. He watched as Gillies knelt at the
small trench they had just dug and pulled soil away with
his hand, working very slowly and delicately.

"Stone," said Gillies at last.

"Yes," said MacAulay.

Gillies bent lower and peered closely at the small area
he had uncovered, removing his glasses in order to do so.

"Dressed too, I would say. Not entirely natural."

He looked up and MacAulay saw a gleam of
excitement in his eyes, the eternal gleam of excitement
common to every treasure hunter who believes he has
finally found the end of the rainbow.

Gillies rose to his feet and fastidiously dusted earth
from the knees of his trousers.

"Of course, we have many of these sites," he said. "Far
too many for our limited resources."

"I understand that," said MacAulay. "But I feel this
one is perhaps different from most."

"It has potential," said Gillies, and in a sudden burst of
frankness unusual in a government servant, he added:
"In fact, I would go further. It has a great deal of
potential."

He went over to the central mound which MacAulay
remembered pointing out to Sneddon. He stood looking
at it for some time and then glanced at the sky.

"I think it might be inadvisable to break this just now. I
wouldn't trust the weather, and we have inadequate
resources for protection. Also, how much to you trust
these people?"

"On Letir-Falloch? The man Sneddon not at all. I have
not yet had a chance to meet the owner and form an
assessment, but his wife seems a good, straightforward
soul."

"Quite. So we need an order from the Secretary of
State, pending a Department offer to purchase the site.
Of course, that may not happen. It will depend what we
find, and there may be insufficient justification for
spending money on opening it up any further."

"I quite understand that. But if you refer to Professor
Stewart Thomson's report in *The Scottish Archaeological*

Review for October 1939 you will find his preliminary observations on the site, which may help to convince the Department."

"Stewart Thompson, eh?" said Gillies in a tone of respect.

"He stayed here the previous fall and found the site, but the war intervened and when it was over Thomson was dead, so nothing further was done and I reckon that memory of the possibilities must have faded."

"Certainly nothing must be done to disturb it until it is properly surveyed," said Gillies, and MacAulay breathed a sigh of relief. That was what he had wanted to hear.

He straightened up himself and as he did so movement from the direction of the house made him turn. A young man was approaching them.

"I think," he said, "we may be about to meet the owner. Mr Shaw?" he asked as the young man came up to them.

"That's me."

"I am very pleased to make your acquaintance at last, sir. I am David MacAulay and this is Mr Gillies of the Department of Ancient Monuments in Edinburgh."

They shook hands, and MacAulay assessed Shaw himself and his mood. He was a very young man, only in his early twenties with a thin pale face and dark hair. He was clearly not very enamoured at having them here, and MacAulay thought it likely that his objections were because of the stopping of his concert.

MacAulay suppressed a pang of envy. He was so young, so immature, and yet by the modern order of things he had been one of the few people who could afford to buy Letir-Falloch from Cousin Astrid's executors, severing a generations-old connection between the MacAulays and their land. It was odd that on the one hand he should disapprove of the privileges of the landed gentry and on the other resent the loss of those privileges by his own kith and kin.

"I very much regret what has happened, Mr Shaw," he went on. "Believe me, I have done my best to contact you for the last week or so, but have found it impossible."

"Because of Sneddon."

"Well —"

"I suppose he was only doing his job. Part of it's to keep

people away from me, but this time he's gone too far."

"It would have saved a lot of unnecessary misunder-
standing had I been able to speak to you directly earlier. I
don't know whether you have been informed about
what we have found here."

"Oh, aye. My wife's been telling me a lot about you,
Mr MacAulay. You're famous in Glendarroch and
Auchtarne."

"Me, sir?"

"Aye. You. Your family used to own Letir-Falloch, is
that right?"

"Well, yes, that is certainly true, but I am a very junior
member of that family —"

"And you were never even let into the house. I'm glad
Sally did something about that."

"I appreciated Mrs Shaw's kindness, sir."

"And you're looking for some kind of ancient
monument, right?"

"That's correct."

"Aye. And you said Mr Gillies comes from somewhere
that deals with them," said Harry Shaw.

"That's it exactly, sir. I was extremely lucky to find it,
in fact. Your man twice tried to remove me from the land
before I finally tracked the site down. Then for some
reason which I don't understand he suddenly agreed to
help. I had thought perhaps his orders had come from
you."

"They didn't. I didn't know anything about you."

"I realised they couldn't have done when I first heard
about your wish to hold a concert here. That was not
until Mr Sneddon informed me this morning."

Harry Shaw nodded.

"I'm beginning to get the picture, I think," he said.
"Sneddon got the job of running Letir-Falloch from my
manager in London. So really he takes his orders from
him. Not from me. And I know Charlie Davenport.
That's my manager. He'd have a pink fit at the idea of me
doing a concert here. Probably has had by now. Sneddon
told him about it, and Charlie told him to put a stop to it.
All that's pretty obvious."

"I regret that it has happened, though."

"That's all right. I've rearranged the concert. It's going

to be in the Auchtarne Town Hall. Pity we can't hold it here. We'd have got more people into the marquee. The Town Hall only hold five hundred. But they tell me the weather's going to break, so maybe it's just as well. Folk wouldn't have been happy walking around here up to their hurdies in sheugh."

MacAulay wasn't quite sure what that meant, but could make a shrewd guess.

"But will your manager approve of a concert in the Auchtarne Town Hall if he disapproves of this one?"

"No. He won't. But it's fixed and Sneddon's probably told him about it by now. Still, with any luck it'll be too late for Charlie to try to stop me. It's going to be on Friday. The day after tomorrow."

"Excellent. I wish you every success with it. A most worthy cause."

"Thanks. And listen, Mr MacAulay, just in case Sneddon changes his mind again, or has it changed for him by Charlie Davenport, you carry on here. Get me? And if Sneddon tries to stop you, tell him I told you so."

"I don't think he will be able to stop anything now anyway, Mr Shaw. Mr Gillies is going to get an order from the Secretary of State for Scotland forbidding damage to this site until it has been properly investigated."

Harry Shaw shrugged his shoulders.

"Fine," he said. "You do that, Mr Gillies. If only I'd known about all this to start with you wouldn't have had to."

He turned and walked away towards the house and MacAulay stood watching him, thinking that perhaps Letir-Falloch hadn't fallen into such bad hands after all.

12

There had been an Olde Tyme Dance in the Town Hall on the Thursday night, so nothing could be started in the way of setting it up for the concert until first thing on the Friday morning, at which time the hall had that old stale smell about it of a place much used for physical activity on a hot summer's night and then closely shut up

for several hours. Furthermore, because the last event in
the hall had been a dance, all the seats were left hard up
against the walls and had to be rearranged.

And the seats were not the most portable things
imaginable. They were metal with red plush upholstery
and they were bolted to boards six in a row. They were
clumsy and awkward to move and each set seemed to
weigh a ton.

Brian had just put down his end of a row of seats in the
right place when he saw Sally Shaw come through the
double doors at the back of the hall and stand there
unobtrusively, watching what was going on.

"Take a spell, Archie, eh?" he suggested and Archie
sank down on to one of the seats they had just put in
place and mopped his forehead with a large handker-
chief.

"Take as long as you like," he said. "I'll go and see
where we can make a cup of tea when I've recovered."

"Always the man to get his priorities right," said
Brian, and he went to the back of the hall and smiled at
Sally.

She smiled tentatively back at him and they stood
watching the activity in the auditorium and on the stage.
Harry was up there talking animatedly to a tall young
man with a mop of fair hair and enormous glasses, who
was dragging boxes of coloured lights on to the stage
from the wings. Elsewhere men were rigging lights,
others were trying to arrange the Town Hall's rather
dingy set of black curtains round the stage to look as rich
and colourful as possible, and the air was filled with the
chatter of voices, the clatter of seats being put into place,
the screech of a Black and Decker attacking a piece of
metal and a carpenter hammering somewhere unseen.

"How's it going?" she asked.

"Fine. Up to time, I'd say." He looked at his watch and
saw that it was already half past ten. "Harry's amazing."

"I'm just frightened he'll be exhausted by tonight."

"I've said that to him but he just laughs."

Harry caught sight of her, waved and jumped off the
stage and came towards them.

"It'd be just like him to break an ankle doing that," she
muttered. "Listen. Before he gets here — I'm on my way

home now. I've got all the stuff to make him a real nice lunch. D'you think someone could bring him back about half past twelve?"

"Sure, I'll do that. So long as he doesn't mind travelling in a van marked Blair's Store."

"Would you? Thanks a lot. Then I'll be sure he actually eats something. And I want him to rest. He thinks he's okay again, but he's still not completely right."

Harry came up to them.

"Hi, Chicken," he said, and he put an arm round her waist, drew her to him and kissed her.

"I'm going home to get a smashing lunch for you, okay?" she said.

He grinned.

"Just like the old days," he said.

"And just like the old days I'm going to make sure you're there to eat it. Mr Blair's promised to bring you back for it. And you're going to eat it, right?"

"She treats me like a baby," he complained to Brian.

"And whiles I've needed to," she said. "And I'm going to chain you to the bed for at least two hours this afternoon."

"I've got too much to do . . . Unless you're going to be there too?" he asked.

"Certainly not. You're going to rest."

"Yes, ma'am. Terrible slave driver, she is," he added to Brian. "Here, I'm glad you put me on to Tommy Sutherland," he went on, nodding at the stage where the tall young man with the glasses was unwinding cable and leading it into the wings. "He's great."

"He's been running the local discos in Auchtarne for years," said Brian. "I don't know much about these things, but to have done it that long he must know what he's up to."

"He does. It's the lights he's useful for because he knows the hall so well. My own roadies will be here in about an hour with the P.A. system. Hey, Tommy!" he shouted to the bespectacled man. "Can you focus that spot higher? It's hitting too low. I'll be further back than that."

He made to hurry off.

"Promise," said Sally. "Half past twelve. No later. I've

asked Mr Blair."

"Cross my heart," he said, doing it. "I can't beat two slave drivers. Get the chains ready."

And he hurried off down the central gangway which was forming as more and more seats were brought in to fill up the auditorium.

"He's in his element," said Brian.

Sally sighed.

"Yes, I'm afraid he is. He's happier today than he's been for ages."

"Well, that can only be good."

"Oh, I'm glad to see it. But I wish —"

She broke off.

"Wish what?"

"Nothing," she said. "You sure you don't mind dragging him away?"

"I'll give him his marching orders at twelve o'clock," Brian promised.

"Thanks."

She smiled fleetingly at him and left the hall and he went back to find that Archie had disappeared in the direction of the gas-ring which he had located in the small and smelly kitchen at the back of the stage.

When they had had a cup of tea and Brian had managed to persuade Archie that they really ought to go and get on, they returned to the hall and went to the back to move out the last of the rows of seats.

They were just finishing when the double doors at the back opened again and a man came into the hall. Brian didn't recognise him, but there was no reason why he should. Auchtarne was big enough not to know everyone by sight, but this stranger seemed very out of place. He was dressed in a light blue suit, a light blue shirt with a rather loudly patterned blue tie and a black Homburg hat sat smartly on top of his glossy black hair. Draped over his shoulders was a brown camel-hair coat which Brian reckoned couldn't have cost less than five hundred pounds.

The man stood there, looking round, smiling a blank smile of disbelief. He caught Brian looking at him and strolled towards him.

"Harry Shaw around?" he asked, and the voice

confirmed that the man was not local. Even with those three words he sounded almost aggressively English.

"Should be," said Brian. "He was here a minute ago." He raised his voice above the din going on around them and shouted "Harry!"

"Hallo!" came an answering shout from somewhere backstage.

"Someone to see you!" shouted Brian.

"Coming!"

Harry appeared a moment later through one of the doors at the side of the stage and came towards the back, an electrician's screwdriver in his hand, calling some instructions over his shoulder to the tall young man with glasses who must still be backstage somewhere. Then he turned and caught sight of the stranger beside Brian and his step faltered for a moment. But only for a moment. With scarcely a pause he put the screwdriver in the pocket of his jeans and came on more slowly and, Brian thought, more deliberately.

"Harry, boy, how's it going?" asked the stranger in a cheerful tone which sounded as false as hell.

"Charlie," said Harry. "I wondered when you'd get here."

"Expect me, did you?"

"Aye. I knew your spy would have told you."

"Course you did," said the stranger approvingly.

He put a hand on Harry's shoulder and patted it and Brian saw Harry flinch away from the gesture.

The stranger looked round. He was out of place here. As out of place as a cat in a bird sanctuary, thought Brian. The clothes, the smoothly shaven cheeks, the sleek black hair and the London accent clashed completely with the slightly faded dinginess of the Victorian hall with its peeling beige walls, the brown curtains covering the mullioned windows and the dark varnished woodwork.

"Listen, Harry, we got to have a chat, boy," said the stranger.

"I don't have to say anything to you, Charlie," said Harry. "I'm still on my holidays, remember."

"Course you are, boy, course you are. That's what I mean. So what's all this, then? You working when you're supposed to be resting, building up your strength? Not good enough, Harry."

"It's good enough for *me*," said Harry.

"Know where I was yesterday? Stuttgart. Come on. I'm gonna tell you things that'll make your hair stand on end. Let's go and grab a cup of coffee, eh? I seen what looked like quite a nice little hotel on my way here. What was it called? The Ocktarn Arms?"

"I haven't time, Charlie. There's a hell of a lot to do before tonight."

"Harry, Harry, give yourself a break. This is your trouble, boy, know what I mean? Always going at things far too hard. Never let up, do you? Relax, boy. Take it easy. Now, come on. I got the car at the door and it's on a yellow line. Didn't know you had them up here in Scotland, but I dessay it'll cost just as much if I get caught, eh?"

His arm was round Harry's shoulder and he was propelling him gently but firmly towards the double doors. Brian saw Harry make an attempt to stop, but the arm was firm and the stranger never stopped talking smoothly and gently, and the door closed behind them with scarcely a sound.

The young man with the fair hair and the glasses came up to Brian.

"Seen Harry?" he asked.

"He's just gone out," said Brian.

"Gone out? But I wanted to try out the limits on the follow spot. Where's he gone?"

"For a cup of coffee, I think."

"By himself?"

"No. With a big bloke in a camel coat that I wouldn't trust further than I could throw him," said Brian thoughtfully, and then added, "which isn't very far, considering his size."

Chapter Five

1

Inverdarroch stopped the tractor and climbed out, taking his piece box and thermos flask with him. It was maybe a little early for a midday meal — his watch showed him that it was only eleven o'clock — but he was suspicious of the weather and he wanted to get the hay cut before it broke down.

Not that stopping an hour early for lunch was going to get it in any faster, but at least by having his midday meal now he would be ready to accelerate should a change in the weather make it necessary.

He settled down in the shade of a sycamore tree at the edge of the field. There was a comfortable soft patch between two roots which he knew of old and he opened the plastic box and looked without much relish at the sandwiches he had hastily prepared before leaving the house at five o'clock that morning. The margarine had oozed out between the slices of bread and one of the chunks of potted meat had slipped against the greasiness of it and had popped out like a pea out of a pod. It didn't look like a pea, though. It was mottled brown and red and wasn't likely to encourage an appetite. He stuffed it back in again, wiped his fingers on the side of his dungarees and began to eat.

The weather might break down later but at the moment it was beautifully sunny and warm. He sat there chewing contentedly, not content with what he was actually eating, but at the blissfulness of the day, listening to the bees busy in the hawthorn hedge behind him and watching the clouds begin to gather over the top of Ben Darroch.

He looked at them with narrowed eyes. Aye, he was right. Two, maybe three hours, and the sun would have gone and there might be rain coming in behind. He mustn't linger too long over his meal.

He finished the food and wiped his fingers again in the same place, feeling glad that the sandwiches had finally gone. They hadn't really been very good. The bread was some days old and it had been like chewing through sawdust. He unscrewed the thermos flask and poured tea into the cup. It was pre-milked and pre-sweetened and it tasted funny and a little metallic from the flask, but it was hot and wet and the heat in the tractor cab and the dry sandwiches had made him very thirsty.

He sat leaning against the trunk of the tree, his cap pushed to the back of his head and closed his eyes for a moment. He was pretty tired, he realised, which was hardly surprising. This was the busiest time of the year when the days were so long, and he had to make the best of them while the weather lasted. There was always the winter in which to do nothing, and he wished that human beings were more like those animals which could sleep all winter and stay awake all summer. Life would be much simpler that way.

He emptied the last of the tea into the cup, drank it down and screwed the cup back on the thermos again. Then he gathered the piece box and pulled himself to his feet.

He had been sitting for ten minutes and that was quite long enough.

As he got up he heard an unusual sound. A slight humming seemed to be approaching. It might almost have been growing out of the background hum of insects all round him, but it was a different noise, and for a moment he stood, head cocked, trying to locate and identify it. A car engine? Possibly, but very quiet if it was.

It was a car engine, and he peered over the top of the hawthorn hedge which came level with his eyes as a brown Rolls Royce rocked and slithered up the track bordering his field and disappeared regally round the next bend. The noise died away again, leaving the insects in sole possession of the day.

Inverdarroch scratched his head and replaced his cap in its proper place.

That was odd.

The cart track, for it was little more, meandered into the hills for a further two and a half miles and ended at the old shooting lodge of Cragganmore. Now in the old days, there might have been activity building up around Cragganmore at this time of the year. The grouse shooting began in a fortnight and for those rich enough and with the peculiar mentality to enjoy slaughtering birds, the servants would by now have been making their way up and down the track, cleaning up the lodge after its long lay-off through the spring and early summer.

But that hadn't happened for years, and so far as he knew Cragganmore Lodge, although still weatherproof, was almost derelict, unvisited and unwanted. It was so remote that even the vandals hadn't found it. The shooting had failed when the birds had mysteriously left the moors and all attempts to reintroduce them artificially had failed, the last of a succession of game-keepers had been given his notice five years ago and since then the place had been deserted.

But here was a brown Rolls Royce heading up the track, and it could only be going to Cragganmore. There was nowhere else.

Inverdarroch shrugged. Well, maybe some rich southerner had taken it into his head to try using a gun up here again. Inverdarroch hoped not, because although by the time the Twelfth came all his hay would be in, he remembered living in constant dread during those later weeks of the summer in the old days when shots sometimes whistled round his ears because of the enthusiasm and lack of accuracy of the parties which had strayed too far from Cragganmore Lodge.

Anyway, there were more important things at the moment, and if he wanted to speculate about what was happening up there he could do it while he worked, and he put the thermos and the piece box in the back of the cab and climbed into the tractor again.

A minute later the engine roared into life and the tractor moved off over the field once more.

2

She looked at her watch for the twentieth time in as many minutes. Or so it seemed. But it was still only twenty-five to one.

She looked round the kitchen. She had spread a cloth at one end of the table and laid cutlery neatly on it and put a vase with a rose from the garden in it in the middle. There were pots standing on the cooker full of tasty things which she had prepared with great care and which smelt very appetising, but which were now growing cold and getting ruined.

Anything might have happened to delay him. She ought to know Harry by now. Once he got enthusiastic about anything time stopped having any meaning, and in the early days of his success when he had left Africa, the group he had started with as lead singer, and gone solo, there had been times when they had literally had to drag him off the stage to stop him. Brian Blair might be having the same trouble getting him away now.

And he wasn't all that late. She'd said twelve-thirty here, after all, and Brian Blair had said he'd make sure he got him away at twelve o'clock, but it would be a fast drive to get here from the Auchtarne Town Hall in half an hour and the traffic might be heavy . . .

Might be. But she had never met really heavy traffic on that road even in the height of summer.

The sight of the neatly laid table and the untouched pots seemed to be mocking her in her anxiety and she left the kitchen, passed through the green baize door into the hall, and wandered restlessly round the house.

She seemed to have spent most of her time doing that for the last few days under different emotional circumstances. Upstairs she opened the door to the drawing room. It was huge and cool and shadowy and she moved restlessly round it. Perhaps because this time MacAulay wasn't with her she felt its alienness more acutely. The huge windows with the heavy plum curtains at them, the immense marble fireplace and the panelled walls hung with hunting and shooting pictures, the faded chintz covers on the deep chairs and sofas and the worn Turkish carpet, acres of it, covering the floor, were all part of a different life. More spacious. More secure. Although it couldn't have been all that secure because it had gone. The house had been bought complete with contents and there was little of their own in it. She had

never been at home here, and now it seemed she was
even less so. She rattled around in Letir-Falloch House
like a pea in a drum, lost in the midst of fifteen bedrooms,
six public rooms and kitchen premises and servants'
quarters which could have held an army. You could
house ten families in the outhouses, too. It seemed all
wrong, and even now that she had the immense relief of
having told Harry about Jimmy and known the
sweetness of true reconciliation, she could not feel
comfortable here.

Harry. Where was he? Of course, Mr Blair might have
stopped at Glendarroch on the way through, but even
so . . .

She looked at her watch again and stood at one of the
drawing room windows, looking down at the gravelled
forecourt which stood in the sunlight empty of traffic
and people.

She went to the door and stepped on to the landing.
There was a gallery which looked down on the stone-
flagged hall where the familiar grandfather clock
continued telling her that she hadn't managed to make
time stand still at all. And all along the corridor on either
side of the gallery, doors led into bedrooms which were
shrouded in dustsheets, unused for years, stuffy in the
heat of summer with their windows all closed.

She heard a cough from the back premises somewhere
and her heart missed a beat. But almost immediately she
realised that it wasn't Harry's cough. It was only
Sneddon in his office.

Come to think of it, he had been hanging about the
house all day, never very far from her sight or hearing. It
was as though he were *aware* of her. That wasn't like him.
He usually ignored her. Why was he doing that?

Was it just her overheated imagination which
immediately led her to think that he was trying to
establish an alibi? That he was making sure she knew he
was here so that she would know that he wasn't doing
anything to Harry?

But if that were so it would mean that he knew
someone else was doing something to Harry. Or was
that making things too complex?

Her impatience boiled over and she hurried down the

wide stairs into the hall. She crossed to the front door, opened it noisily, held it for a moment and then slammed it shut.

She waited.

The green baize door at the back of the hall opened and Sneddon's head appeared. He saw her standing there looking at him, and he actually seemed a little uncomfortable.

"Thought I heard you go out," he said, the first time he had ever taken the trouble to explain his actions to her. That in itself confirmed her suspicions.

"I'm just going *now*," she said, and she went, this time closing the door behind her.

She stood there letting the sun beat down on her while she frowned, trying to work it out. He had been waiting there, deliberately keeping an eye on her.

Why?

Well, she wouldn't get any answer out of Sneddon. If she were going to get one at all it would be at the Town Hall in Auchtarne.

3

Archie sat down beside Eddie with a thump on one of the seats they had put up for the audience that night. He took off his cap and wiped his forehead with the back of his arm.

"Tired, Archie?" asked Eddie as he unwrapped his packet of sandwiches. He had come up to the Town Hall from the pier when he brought the midday ferry in to see how things were going and ask if he could lend a hand, but he had found that preparations were well advanced and in fact he was not needed. All that remained to be done was technical stuff where none of them could be of much help, except possibly in the field of fetching and carrying, so he thought he would just sit here and have his lunch before going back to the pier to take the ferry over to Glendarroch again later in the afternoon.

Everything seemed to have slowed down and stopped for a lunch break and the hall was surprisingly empty and echoing after the activity of the morning.

"Listen," said Archie, speaking from the heart, "I used to think working at the Big House was tough. You know me, Eddie. If I start something I give it everything I've got."

"I've noticed," said Eddie.

"But this beats all. Do you know, I've only had one cup of tea since the last one?"

"Aw! And when was the last one?"

"The last one was at eleven o'clock," said Archie in an aggrieved tone.

"And when was the one after that?"

"You mean the last last one? About a quarter to twelve, I think."

"Never mind," said Eddie. "It looks as if you must be just about finished here."

"We are," said Archie. "And am I glad. Here, Eddie — lend us one of your sandwiches?"

"Lend it? You mean you're going to give it back?"

"I'll try to get out to buy some at the baker's in a minute. It's just to give me strength to get across the road."

"All right," said Eddie, handing him the package which Sheila had made up for him that morning.

Archie examined the contents with some distaste.

"Only sardine?" he asked.

"Sorry. I like sardines," said Eddie.

"Oh, well. No accounting for tastes, I suppose," said Archie taking one and experimenting with a mouthful. He chewed for a moment and then nodded. "Not bad," he said grudgingly. "You've got a good woman there, Eddie."

"I know I have."

"She can make a sandwich."

"There's more to her than just making sandwiches."

Bob came down the gangway from the double doors at the back.

"Know what?" he said when he saw them. "There are people starting to queue outside already."

"There you are, Archie," said Eddie. "It's all been worth while."

"Well, we did say first come first served, but this is ridiculous," said Archie. "Queuing already? It's not one o'clock yet. Six and a half hours. People have no sense."

"It probably means a full house, anyway," said Eddie. "And that's what matters as far as the lifeboat's concerned." He scrunched up the paper which had been round his sandwiches and looked for a plastic bag to put it in. "Don't worry about the sandwich, Archie," he said pointedly. "I'll get it from you some other time. If this afternoon's ferry never gets back to Glendarroch you'll probably find me floating somewhere in the loch dead of starvation."

Brian walked on to the stage and Archie burst into applause.

"Do it again," he shouted. "I missed it."

But Brian didn't respond.

"Any of you seen Harry Shaw?" he asked, standing on the stage and addressing anyone who might be within hearing.

"Not for an hour or so," said Bob.

"I promised his wife I'd give him a lift home for some food and a rest at twelve o'clock. I've been looking for him for twenty minutes and can't find him anywhere."

"He's probably gone with someone else," said Eddie.

"I don't think so. He knew I was going to run him back—"

At that moment the double doors at the back burst open and Sally Shaw came hurrying in.

"Where's Harry?" she asked.

There was an ominous silence.

"I've been looking for him for half an hour. He's not here," said Brian.

"Then where is he?"

"We were wondering if someone else had given him a lift back to Letir-Falloch without telling me."

"Do you think I'd be here if he'd come back to Letir-Falloch?" said Sally, her voice taut with anxiety. "I've just come from there and I didn't pass him on the way. You said you'd bring him back."

"Well, maybe he's gone for a quick one before lunch. Goodness knows he was working hard enough earlier on. Even harder than me," said Archie.

"Harry never drinks on the day of a concert," she said. "Not till it's over."

That same ominous silence descended once more, and Eddie felt the tension build up.

"Who saw him last?" he asked.

"I have an idea I did," said Brian. "When that bloke arrived and went off with him for a cup of coffee at the Auchtarne Arms."

"What bloke went off with him?" demanded Sally, her voice suddenly shrill.

"I don't know who he was. London accent. Big, burly bloke with smooth black hair and expensive clothes."

Eddie saw her face turn pale suddenly and she sat down on a nearby seat as though her legs would no longer carry her.

"God. Charlie Davenport," she said.

"Who's Charlie Davenport when he's at home?"

"He's Harry's manager."

"Come to think of it, Harry did refer to him as Charlie," said Brian thoughtfully.

"Oh. Well that's all right, isn't it?" said Bob.

She looked at each of them in turn and her eyes were haggard.

"You don't know Charlie Davenport," she said. "Charlie was dead against the idea of Harry doing this concert and if he's come all the way up here from London he's going to make certain he doesn't do it."

4

Harry's working relationship with Charlie Davenport had always been a strange one. On the one hand he appreciated the way Charlie had, right from the start, taken the weight of organisation off his shoulders, had handled all the infuriating details of bookings and travel and legal problems, of accommodation and supporting acts and backing groups and musicians and above all had negotiated contracts and had, in fact, been responsible for making Harry more money than he had ever dreamt existed before he had thrown up his job and taken the plunge into the dangerous and uncertain world of pop music. For that he owed Charlie a lot.

But he couldn't like him, could never think of him as a friend. Charlie's background was much the same as his own, but whereas Harry saw nothing wrong in his, nothing to be ashamed of and no need to try to change it, Charlie seemed determined to show how high he had risen in the world, to parade his talents and his money for all to see, to wear enormously expensive clothes, to exhibit his advancement and his financial success. And the result was that Charlie was not genuine. You couldn't believe him and you couldn't believe *in* him, and while his display of friendliness and concern always *seemed* genuine, the thought was always lurking at the back of your mind that once you set foot on the slippery downward slope, Charlie would abandon you to the wolves without a second thought.

And Harry certainly didn't trust him now. To begin with they hadn't gone anywhere near the Auchtarne Arms for the coffee Charlie had talked about. Instead they had stepped out of the Town Hall and Charlie's arm had still been on his elbow as he guided him down the steps and into the brown Rolls Royce which stood waiting at the foot.

Harry had protested that it was less than a hundred yards to walk to the hotel, but Charlie had laughed his rich laugh and said he never walked anywhere when he could drive. They had stepped into the spacious interior of the car and Harry had sunk back on the cushions and watched as the silent chauffeur in full uniform with black gloves had started the engine and the car had moved silently and effortlessly out into the Auchtarne High Street and slid smoothly away out of the town, almost as though he were watching a television set with the sound turned down.

"Where are we going?" Harry had asked, feeling a surge of panic rising in him.

"Just somewhere we can talk, Harry. Somewhere I know of. Nothing to worry about, boy."

"I've got to be back soon —"

"And you will be, I promise you."

"D'you mean that?"

Charlie spread his hands.

"Harry," he said plaintively, "have you ever known me break my word?"

Harry was silent. He couldn't think of a time when he had, but then Charlie had such a line of patter that it was difficult to remember what he had said at any given time.

The car left Auchtarne behind and gathered speed along the road.

"Now, listen —" said Harry, looking round desperately for some means of getting out. Every minute was taking him further from the Town Hall and from the concert which he was determined should take place that night.

Bill and Ben would be there soon. They'd be on their way from Glasgow, probably in that same old beat-up blue van, with the P.A. gear. They knew what he wanted because when he'd spoken to them the other day he'd said it would be just like one of the gigs they'd done in and around Glasgow in the old days. He'd spoken to Bill the first time he'd rung and to Ben the second when he'd had to tell them of the change of date and venue from Letir-Falloch on Saturday to Auchtarne on Friday, and each of them had said, "Nae bother, Harry", and he knew it wouldn't be and that they'd quietly get everything set up whether he was there or not. But he should be there. And he wasn't.

"Relax, Harry. Don't you go getting all worked up. It's bad for you."

Charlie sat back in his seat, crossed his legs and produced a cigar case from his inside jacket pocket. He held it out to Harry, knowing perfectly well that he didn't smoke. Harry shook his head impatiently and turned to look out of the window as Charlie selected one for himself, lit up and the rich smell of cigar tobacco rolled round the back of the Rolls Royce.

A little later the car turned off the main road and the smooth ride was at an end. The springs and shock absorbers couldn't cushion all the bumps and irregularities of the road they were on now. Road? It wasn't a road. It was little more than a track, so narrow that every now and again the bushes on either side brushed against the paintwork of the Rolls.

"Where are we going?" asked Harry.

"Place called Cragganmore Lodge," said Charlie.

"Yours?" asked Harry, and Charlie laughed.

"Mine?" he said. "Not on your life, boy. What would I do with a pad in a place like this? Nothing to do.

Nowhere to go. No, like I always tell you, Harry, in this life it's not what you know, it's who you know. Remember when I got you Letir-Fallock? Chap in the estate agents that handled that's a good friend of mine. He put me on to this."

"How long are you staying?"

Charlie looked at him through the cigar smoke, smiled and didn't answer directly.

"Shouldn't take us long now," he said.

The track wound up the hillside. The bushes became stunted and then disappeared and the ground broke away into a wide sweep of moorland on all sides with the distant hills blue beyond. The heather was just beginning to turn purple, but it would be another month before it reached its full glory. At the moment only patches of it stood out from the general brown colour.

There were no houses and Harry shivered involuntarily. All his life he had been used to people and buildings around him. Even Letir-Falloch, which over the last few days had become something of a haven, always gave you the feeling that there were people within call. There were roofs and chimneys to be seen from the upstairs windows. You weren't completely alone.

Here the kindly cultivated country had gone. This was empty, primal, unchanged for centuries, virtually unknown to man.

He wished they might meet another car coming in the opposite direction. There were no passing places, and they would have to stop, perhaps reverse all the way back again. Then at least he would have the chance to get out and escape . . .

Why was he thinking of escape? Charlie was his manager, for heaven's sake. What was there to escape from? He didn't know the answer to that question and wasn't sure that he wanted one.

The car rocked on and then suddenly they breasted a slight rise and in the hollow beyond lay a house. It was low and rambling, solid grey stone, grey-roofed with a crop of outbuildings at the back, and as they drew nearer Harry could see a general air of neglect about the place. The rones and the waste pipes needed painting. So did the windows and the front door where the white paint was cracked and peeling. A glass-roofed portico ran the length of the front of the house, supported on rusting iron pillars, and several of the panes of glass were cracked.

The car swung in a circle over the weed-encrusted forecourt and drew to a halt at the door.

"Come on, Harry," said Charlie. "Welcome to the country estate."

Harry got out on his own side, wondering whether he oughtn't to make a run for it, but then where would he go without transport? In any case when he stepped out the chauffeur was already standing at the door, blocking any escape.

Charlie ushered him towards the door which opened as they reached it. A man with a broken nose and small eyes stood there. He had a short, thickset body and a bull neck, short stubby but immensely strong fingers and fists the size of hams, and the whole aspect screamed at Harry the one word *Bouncer*. He'd seen this man duplicated many times at every concert he'd done. The men in the tight shiny dinner jackets and the squint bow ties, expressionless and watchful, who patrolled the aisles waiting for trouble and stopping it when it arose.

A few quiet words passed between Charlie and the Bouncer, but Harry was so concerned with the new impressions opening up around him and the growing worry of what it all meant that by the time he thought of trying to listen the conversation was over and it was too late.

The door closed behind him, shutting out the outside world. The house smelt stale and musty and Harry noticed the Calor gas heaters in the hall, heaters which should have been unnecessary after the weather they had been having in these parts. The house must have been disused for a very long time and the damp must have penetrated deeply for these to be necessary, and in fact there seemed to be a chill in the air, though that might simply have been the rising tide of fear which he felt inside.

He was conscious of dust lying all over everything, so he had no clear impression of the furniture, only of a uniform grey pall.

The Bouncer led the way to a door and flung it open and Charlie ushered him into the room beyond.

The furniture was old and had at one time been good, but there were many obvious signs of neglect. The tapestry seat of a chair in the window was badly frayed. The curtains were streaked where the sunlight had faded them as they hung there. And there was the smell of must and the sickly smell of Calor gas mingled with it.

"Got any lunch, Syd?" asked Charlie and the Bouncer nodded and disappeared.

Charlie laid his cigar down in an ashtray on the mantelpiece and turned to Harry. He hadn't yet taken off his coat.

"Sit down, Harry," he said cheerfully. "Let's have something to eat, eh? I'm so hungry I could eat a horse. With Syd on the job, that's probably what we'll get." He laughed heartily at his own joke. "Must be something about the air here. My stomach feels as if my throat's been cut. How about you?"

Harry shook his head, not trusting himself to speak, his mind busy with dark thoughts. This house which Charlie had — hired, he supposed. He must have spent a small fortune in getting people up here to put it in some sort of order. Everything spoke of hasty attempts to make the place habitable, and Charlie's own trip in his own chauffeur-driven car, probably overnight from London to Auchtarne, betokened something very big indeed going on, and whatever it was, Harry was pretty sure it wasn't good.

"This place on the telephone?" he asked, trying to sound casual. "I'd better call Sally and tell her where I am."

Charlie spread his hands again apologetically.

"Sorry, Harry. No phone. I don't think there ever has been, and even if there was it wouldn't be connected no more."

That wasn't too good either, though not altogether unexpected.

Syd the Bouncer opened the door and came in with a tray. Harry saw packets of chicken and salad, a bottle of Niersteiner, a couple of cans of export and a couple of lager, and some sort of pink frothy-looking pudding. All this must have been bought prepacked in Auchtarne. Or maybe London. He wondered if there were even any electricity in the places. There was a switch at the door and there were plugs beside the fireplace, but nothing was plugged into them and the light wasn't on. There was probably an unusable generator in an outhouse, he thought. There could be no mains this far from civilisation.

The whole set up seemed very temporary indeed.

"Thanks, Syd. Can you lay on some coffee later?"

Syd nodded. A man of few words, thought Harry, and wished he would say something. It might be interesting to know where he came from.

Charlie got to work with the corkscrew as Syd went out and closed the door quietly behind him.

"Dunno what this is like, Harry. It isn't chilled, I'm afraid. Like some, or will you stick to beer?"

Harry shook his head.

"You know I don't drink before a concert," he said.

Charlie nodded sympathetically as he drew the cork and poured some of the wine into a plastic glass.

"Course you don't. Fancy me forgetting. But listen, Harry. This little concert of yours. It's not a good idea, know what I mean?"

"I didn't think you'd like it, Charlie."

"I don't. What's it all about, boy?"

It would have to be explained, of course, but Harry wasn't sure that he could make Charlie understand. Come to think of it, he didn't altogether understand himself.

"You know I got into trouble a few days ago?" said Harry.

"I heard about your little problem, yes."

"From Sneddon, I suppose."

Charlie sat down and began to unwrap one of the prepackaged chicken and salads on the tray.

"What do you eat this stuff with?" he asked nobody in particular. "Oh, here we are. Ruddy plastic. Oh, well. Yes, I heard about that, Harry. You should of taken more care of yourself, boy."

"Well, I was taken care of by the local lifeboat. They

saved my life."

"Good for them."

"And the lifeboat's run by the locals. Not the proper Lifeboat people. It has to pay its own way. And they haven't got any money."

"They want money, I'll write them a cheque. How much do you think, Harry? A hundred? Five hundred? Just you say."

Harry shook his head.

"That's no good, Charlie. I could do that myself. It's not enough."

"A thousand would be pushing it a bit."

"It's not the amount. That's not the point."

"Then what is the point, Harry?"

Harry was silent, not finding it easy to put into words, but suddenly knowing that it was desperately important to convince Charlie he was right.

"Come on, boy. You can tell me. You know that."

"They got themselves into danger rescuing me, and they got the lifeboat damaged," said Harry. "They weren't thinking of money at the time, any more than I was. But I — well — I just feel that I've got to do something *myself*, to repay them. Do you see what I mean?"

"Very noble, Harry."

"It's not frigging noble, Charlie. It's just — it's just the only way I can feel easy in my mind again after what they did for me."

"But not a concert, Harry."

"Why not? It's the only thing I can do."

"Look, Harry, try to take the long view." Charlie picked up the chicken leg and gnawed at it for a minute, then wiped his fingers fastidiously on the paper napkin provided with the plastic tray and sat back chewing. "This music world of ours, Harry. It's a funny one. You just got back from America. Now I know you had trouble there and I appreciate that you had to ditch the tour and come home otherwise you might of had a real break-down, and that's why I suggested you come up here and have a nice holiday with the little woman, eh? And in a way, you cutting the tour short may not of been a bad thing. Got a lot of publicity out of it. Well, while you've been convalescing I got started on what we do next, know what I mean? Now, that last single of yours. *What Will You Do To Me Next?* It's going big in Europe. We got to cash in on that, and like I told you, I've been trying to fix you a European tour. Well, I got it, Harry. Finally fixed it in Stuttgart yesterday. You and me, we sign it Wensday. And it's a good one, Harry. You'll like it. Don't say I don't look after you, boy." He began to tick off the advantages on beautifully manicured fingers. "Only two concerts a week, never more than eight hours travel between venues, and I've got a guarantee that you won't be asked to do more than twenty minutes at each of them. Now, all that wasn't easy, Harry, seeing as you're still fairly new in Europe."

"Charlie, I know all that —"

"So things is delicate, Harry. Put yourself in the position of one of these European backers. Suppose we've just tied up the deal, it's waiting for signature and this guy's worried about how much money he's got to lay out, he's edgy, know what I mean? Then he suddenly hears that the great star he's spending so much lolly on is doing a cruddy concert in the Scotch backwoods in a dirty old Town Hall to an audience of five hundred. Well, I ask you. What's he going to think, Harry? I'll tell you, boy. He's going to think, this guy's not so hot as that geyser Davenport was making out. These managers, they're all the same, he says to himself. Sell you a stuffed penguin if they get the chance. This guy, he can't be no good, if he's got to do something like that. Don't sign the contract. Get Tom, or Dick instead of Harry. That's what he's thinking. Now, you know me, Harry. I'm a reasonable man, and if you'd fixed this little soiree of yours for *next* Saturday I wouldn't of minded at all, because by then the deal would be signed and sealed and they couldn't of wriggled out of it, know what I mean?"

Harry was silent, thinking. Outside the sun had suddenly gone in and the room had become even darker and dingier than it was before. He realised that all Charlie was saying was true and that he didn't really care. That surprised him. He remembered the excitement he had felt when Charlie had announced the finalisation of the American tour. He knew that Charlie had been wheeling and dealing away at a possible European tour, and he'd felt excited at that too. But something had happened since that illness in America and also since the accident on the loch. Maybe he was being more realistic now, but the tour held no attraction for him. There was no excitement in it. He hadn't even asked Charlie about the money, but he knew that whatever Charlie told him it was, it wouldn't make him gasp in amazement. It all seemed unreal and unimportant, much less real and much less important than this little soirée in Charlie's Scotch backwoods. He knew Charlie didn't like the idea of Harry doing this concert tonight, and he had told him his reasons, which Harry realised were valid ones from Charlie's point of view. And what Charlie didn't want him to do, Charlie would make sure he didn't do.

"Funny thing, you know, Charlie," he said. "It doesn't matter to me now. What happened to me in America gave me a new angle on things. Then on the loch the other day I knew I was right. This concert tonight's more important to me than any European tour. Or the American one either."

Charlie looked at him as if he'd blasphemed in church.

"Harry, boy, you don't know what you're saying," he said.

"Aye, I do. What I'm saying is that what happened in America and on the loch has put all this high-powered stuff in its proper place."

"This high-powered stuff, as you call it, has made you a lot of money," said Charlie.

"It damned nearly lost me my wife," said Harry quietly, suddenly seeing that that was what concerned him most. He had nearly lost Sally, in fact he had nearly driven her away from him. Now he wanted her back with him, and that was what mattered, and if he never earned another penny from singing it didn't matter a tuppeny damn so long as she was there and they could share their lives together.

Charlie smiled at him disbelievingly.

"Just a minute, boy," he said. "You're not trying to say you want to give it all up and go back to being a bloody electrician?"

"Thanks for suggesting it, Charlie," he said slowly.

"It's not a bad idea. At least I'd be my own man there."

Charlie put the bare chicken bone carefully on the cardboard plate and wiped his fingers on the paper napkin.

"Harry, you know you've got a three-year contract with me," he said. His voice had gone rather quiet, and the friendly bantering tone it had had up till now was missing.

"I know that."

"And you know it's still got nearly eighteen months to run."

"I know that too."

"Well, then, I'm glad you're being sensible, boy."

"But I also know that after what happened to me in America it wouldn't be hard to find a doctor who'd say that I'm not fit to complete it."

Charlie's eyes narrowed and looked rather ugly for a moment, and then he suddenly laughed.

"God, boy, I didn't know you had it in you. You're learning."

Harry looked at him seriously.

"I've had a good teacher," he said. "And I'm going to do that concert, Charlie."

Charlie shook his head and peeled the top off the pink fluffy-looking pudding, smelt it warily and poked at it with a plastic spoon.

"No, boy, you're not," he said.

"You can't stop me."

Charlie sighed and took a mouthful of the pink fluffy stuff and made a grimace of distaste.

"I'm afraid I can, Harry. I hoped this wouldn't be necessary, but it was one of the reasons I took the house. You're staying here, Harry."

That was it, out in the open at last, and in a way it was a relief. Harry wasn't good at verbal fencing, because that was Charlie's job, not his. And now that it was over it was no surprise.

But the relief was tinged with coldness.

"Kidnapping, Charlie?" he said.

"Course not. People only kidnap people when they want to make some money. There's no money in this, Harry. No, you're just staying here as my guest. Till tomorrow morning."

"You promised —"

"Sure. I promised you'd be back soon. Tomorrow morning's soon, isn't it?"

"Not soon enough."

"Oh, well, we didn't go into details, did we?"

He smiled at Harry who felt the coldness grow. He sprang to his feet, ready to run for the door, but Charlie called suddenly:

"Syd!"

And the door opened so promptly that the Bouncer must have been waiting just outside.

There were two of them. Syd, the original, and one who might well have been his twin brother hovering in the background, and Harry realised that there wasn't the remotest hope of getting past them to the open air outside.

5

"Mrs Shaw, please sit down and try to relax."

The interview room at the Auchtarne Police Station had its walls covered with posters exhorting the public to do this and that and the next and not to do the other, the main advantage being that they hid most of the sickly official green paint in which the room was predominantly decorated. The metal-framed windows had frosted glass in them and the hard square wooden chairs were distinctly uncomfortable.

Sergeant Murray looked at the girl who sat bolt upright in the chair opposite him. She was trembling all over and her fingers were clasped and never still. She was overwrought, he thought, and he would have to deal with her very gently.

"Now let me get this straight," he said. "Your husband is a singer, right?"

She nodded.

"And he goes under the name of Vincent?"

She nodded again.

"Aye. I've heard tell of him," said Sergeant Murray noncommittally. He consulted his notebook. "Now, he has been preparing for a concert in the Town Hall this evening. At some time in the course of the morning he was accosted by someone purporting to be his manager and he went off with him and hasn't been seen since."

She nodded again.

Sergeant Murray tapped his teeth with his ballpoint pen, feeling slightly baffled.

"Aye. Well, there doesn't seem to me to be anything unusual in all this, Mrs Shaw. You yourself say it was your husband's manager so we must assume for the sake of argument that it was. Though, come to think of it, we have no proof of that."

"No one else knows Charlie Davenport, but the description the other people in the hall gave me fits," she said.

"Well, anyway, that's easy enough to check just by ringing his office in London and asking where he is," said Murray. "But the point that worries me, Mrs Shaw, is this. This happened — when? Eleven o'clock? Half past eleven this morning?"

"No one can remember the exact time."

"Aye, it's a pity folk in real life aren't so definite about the time as they are in these detective novels," said Sergeant Murray. "But whatever, it's not all that long ago. There doesn't seem to me to be anything suspicious about a singer going away to have a long chat with his manager and perhaps forgetting about a lunch appointment, especially if, as you say, there's some big deal coming up which could mean a lot of work and money for him."

"But I know that's not what Charlie's here for," said Mrs Shaw desperately. "I *know* it, Sergeant! Anything like that could have waited till we were back in London next week. Or he could have talked to Harry on the telephone. Charlie's not the man to drive all the way up here without some very good reason."

"Aye, aye, well, it seems to me that we can't be very certain what the reason might be at the moment," he said. "But from an outsider's point of view it doesn't seem likely that he'd have come all this way to kidnap your husband just to stop him from doing a concert."

"But he *has*, Sergeant!"

She stared at him pleadingly, begging him to
understand and Sergeant Murray felt a flash of
sympathy for her. The girl was worried, there was no
doubt of that, but really that might be the reason why
she had come here. Overwrought wife worried about
her husband's health, building mountains out of
molehills . . . Sergeant Murray had had hysterical
customers before and no doubt would have them again.

It would be best to try to soothe her.

"I'll tell you what I'll do," he said. "There's not enough
evidence here to start a full-scale search, or register your
husband as a missing person. Not after just a couple of
hours, anyway. What I can do is put out an alert to ask
everyone on the beat to keep an eye open for him, now
how would that be? If there's no sign of him by this
evening, then we'll set things in motion, and with this
kind of advance warning we can do that very quickly."

"But don't you see, this evening will be too late! I'm
sure he'll be back by tomorrow morning. But Charlie's
going to make sure he's not around to do the concert."

"I'm sure you're just worrying too much about him,
Mrs Shaw. Mind you, I'm not saying that's a bad thing at
all." He got up. "I sometimes wish my wife made half as
much fuss about me," he added with what he hoped
would be a fatherly smile. "Now, you just go home, Mrs
Shaw, and try not to worry. I tell you what I think. I
think you'll find your husband waiting there for you,
and I just hope he's not thinking of calling the police and
reporting *you* missing."

6

"So they didn't go to the Auchtarne Arms for coffee,"
said Brian.

Bob shook his head.

"I saw them get into this brown Rolls Royce," he said.
"That was just before I came in and told you there were
people beginning to queue already. And they haven't
been at the Auchtarne Arms. The receptionist there has
been on duty all morning and she knows Vincent. She's a
fan. And she says she'd have recognised him even if he'd

come in in a beard and dark glasses and she'd have asked
him for his autograph."

"So where have they gone?" muttered Brian.

"You think Sally Shaw may be right?"

"I didn't. But now I'm beginning to wonder. He hasn't
been seen for two hours now."

"And meanwhile that queue's reached the corner of
the Town Hall. There must be a hundred and fifty people
out there."

The Town Hall seemed to be holding its breath. True,
it was still an official lunch hour which wouldn't end till
two o'clock, but there was a silence about the place
which seemed unnatural. Almost as if the hall itself were
waiting.

As certainly all the people were. The electricians were
gathered in a corner talking in low voices, obviously
wondering if there was any point in going on rigging the
lights. Tommy Sutherland was wandering on and off the
stage like a lost soul. The whole impetus there had been
earlier that morning had gone with the loss of the main
driving force, and the men from Glasgow had not yet
arrived with the P.A. system.

"And where's Sally?" asked Bob.

"At the police station," said Brian.

Bob whistled silently.

"Does she think that's going to do any good?"

"She'll be hoping so. But I don't think it will."

"What do we do?"

Brian shrugged his shoulders.

"Search me," he said.

At that moment there was a crash which shattered the
stillness in the hall as the doors at the back of the
auditorium were thrown open and Sally hurried in. She
caught sight of the two of them sitting halfway down
the aisle and came running towards them.

"They won't do anything," she said.

"Well, what could they do?" asked Brian.

"They could at least try to find him," she said, her
voice rising to a high-pitched squeak.

"Steady," said Brian, gripping her arm, but she
shrugged him off.

"How can I?" she asked. "No one seems to believe me.

Charlie Davenport's kidnapped Harry. I know he has!"

"I don't understand why he would do that," said Brian.

She stood breathing heavily for a moment and then she made a determined effort to calm down and speak rationally.

"Look, Charlie makes a lot of money out of Harry, right?" she said.

"I suppose he must do."

"And he wants to make as much as he can, right?"

"Looking at him, I can believe that."

"And can you believe that Charlie wouldn't worry too much about how Harry was so long as he was making him money?"

"Yes, I think I can believe that."

"Charlie got Sneddon to knock the Letir-Falloch concert on the head, right?"

"So we're told."

"That's what happened, believe you me. Now Sneddon's told Charlie about this one and Charlie's come here himself to put a stop to it too."

"But why?"

Sally sighed.

"It's the business," she said. "Things change fast in the pop world. Star today, forgotten tomorrow. Have you got any idea how long the average pop star's life of fame is?"

"It's not something that's ever crossed my mind," said Brian.

"Three years. If you get three years out of it at the top you're doing very well. Oh, there are exceptions. Rod Stewart, Cliff Richard, The Stones. But there are very few of them. So, when Charlie gets a top star he's going to milk him for every penny he can while he can, because it'll all soon be over, right?"

Brian nodded.

"Harry's been at the top for eighteen months now. He's halfway through his life."

"Do you think so?"

"I know so. It's not just that the fans get tired of you. You get tired of the fans. The whole mad world starts going stale on you. And thank God, that's started to happen with Harry. He doesn't care about it any longer.

Charlie's been trying to fix a European tour for him, and that'll probably be the last big thing that'll happen to him."

"I don't see what all this has to do with him not wanting Harry to do this concert tonight. After all, he's doing it for a good cause."

"Do you honestly think that the Glendarroch lifeboat's going to mean a thing to some stinking rich German businessman in Frankfurt? *He's* not going to understand why Harry's wasting his time on a tiny gig in Auchtarne."

Brian thought about the Germans he had known in the days when the Glendarroch estate had been owned by them, and he realised that she was right. Without exception they had been utterly self-centred, utterly uncaring and utterly unscrupulous.

"And Charlie knows that. He wants another year or two of a percentage off Harry. He's been working very hard to get it and he's probably laid out a lot of money on it and he's not going to throw it away now."

"But Harry's been ill," said Bob.

"Think that worries Charlie?" Sally rounded on him. "Of course it doesn't. Charlie got Harry to come up here. I didn't like the idea because —" She glanced guiltily at Brian and then looked away again "— well, you know why I wasn't keen to come back. But Charlie wouldn't listen to me. Why should he? I'm not a valuable property like Harry is. Get Harry up here for some peace and quiet. That's what he said. Get him better as quick as you can before people forget him and so that Charlie can get this deal pushed through. That's what he meant. Keep Harry going for three months or however long this European tour lasts for and after that it doesn't matter. He can go away and die then if he wants to. There won't be much more to be made out of him anyway. Another couple of singles might get into the top twenty, but after that it's all over, and the search'll be on for the next bright young hopeful to take Harry's place for three years before he or she gets burnt out and thrown on the scrap heap too."

Brian grunted.

"Sounds like a real exciting, friendly world."

"It might be if it wasn't for the Charlie Davenports in it."

"So what do you suggest we do?"

"Listen, Harry wants to do this concert. I've never known him so keen to do anything in his life. It really means a lot to him. I thought he was crazy trying to organise it so quickly, and I still think he is, but we'll be away by the middle of next week so it's now or never. And as he feels like that I want him to succeed. And I wouldn't mind doing Charlie Davenport in the eye at the same time."

She put her hands on her hips and looked at the pair of them defiantly.

"You want this concert?"

They nodded.

"Then as the police aren't going to do anything about it, the only thing we can do is find a brown Rolls Royce pretty damned quick," she said.

7

"Syd and Algy done a good job here, Harry. All the comforts of home, you might say."

Harry stood in the master bedroom and looked around. It was a big room. There was a large double bed and there were fresh sheets and pillowcases on it. There was a huge fireplace in which a Calor gas heater stood, though it seemed to have been turned off. A couple of huge and comfortable looking armchairs stood on either side of it. There was no television set, but on a side table stood a large battery radio cassette player and a pile of magazines and cassettes. Harry recognised a couple of his own and wondered if Charlie really thought he was going to sit here for hours twiddling his thumbs and listening to them. There was a heavy dark bedroom suite with carvings of fruit all over it, and there were little tables and stools. All very opulent. The surfaces had been dusted, but Harry could see that the skirting board was still thick with it, and so were the tops of the picture frames on the walls. Years of Sally's houseproud spirit had taught him to notice these things. Sally. Where was she now and what was she doing and was she worrying? He knew she would be and suddenly he longed for her with a terrible longing which the thought of what she would have said about the way this room had been cleaned made all the worse.

And the room was musty. The windows were tightly closed.

"You expect me to stay in here till tomorrow, do you?" he asked.

"Harry, boy, it's for your own good. Long term. You'll live to thank me. Honest."

Harry made a derisory noise.

"I'd give you the freedom of the house, but we got a staff shortage, know what I mean? Besides, you'll be comfortable in here. At least it's the warmest place I come across in this Scotch weather. It's the best room in the house, too. Syd and Algy seen to that. All the comforts of home. Just one thing. There's no point ringing the bell. It doesn't work. But all you got to do is shout. Syd or Algy'll be around to give you anything you want, right?"

"Except freedom," said Harry.

Charlie patted him encouragingly on the back.

"You'll have all the freedom you want in just a few hours, believe me, Harry. First thing tomorrow the boys will see you safe back to Letir-Fallock. After that you can do what you like. Go where you like. Just so long as you're back in London Wednesday to sign that contract, you do your own thing, boy. Right?"

Charlie patted him on the shoulder and left the room. The two Bouncers followed him and the door closed. Harry listened and heard the key turn in the lock and when he tried the handle the door wouldn't open.

He felt anger begin to take over from fear. Whatever Charlie said about being free in just a few hours, this was kidnap.

He went to the window. It was an ordinary sash window with fairly small panes of glass and Harry noticed a mortice lock on it. That was unusual, and it wasn't new, so it hadn't been part of Syd and Algy's preparations for entertaining him. Probably some previous owner had had it set there so that during the

long months in the year when the house was
unoccupied, anything valuable could be locked into the
one room. That and Cragganmore Lodge's distance from
civilisation would make it quite safe. He looked out. The
sun had gone completely now and the hills in the
distance seemed to have disappeared in a kind of grey
haze. You could see across the forecourt and to the edge
of the moorland, but no further. It was rather as though
the lodge were sitting in a world which was rapidly
getting smaller and from which the colour was being
drained.

Through the glass of the canopy just below the
window he could see the Rolls Royce still standing there,
and after a moment he saw Charlie appear underneath
him. He paused at the door of the car and turned,
obviously to say something to one or other of the
Bouncers still in the house, his black hair glossy and
gleaming even without the aid of sunlight, and then he
stepped in, the door closed and the car glided across the
forecourt and vanished along the track which wound
downwards from the house to the green land and the
activity and the friends down there, and Harry felt very
alone.

There had been no sound through the window, but
now he heard the front door close and the sound of
footsteps below. He thought he detected one set going
towards the back of the house, and then he heard a stair
creak and realised that the other set was coming closer.
A door opened not far away in the corridor and didn't
close again, the footsteps stopped and there was the
creak of bedsprings. One of the Bouncers had obviously
taken up a guard post, ready and waiting for his shout to
provide whatever it was he wanted. Except, thought
Harry, a way out to Auchtarne in time for the concert.

8

Dougal stared at Brian in disbelief.
"Kidnapping?" he echoed.
Brian nodded.
"That's what she thinks," he said, "and the longer time

goes on and there's no sign of him the more likely it looks."

Dougal glanced at his mother and saw his own disbelief mirrored in her face.

"Things like that just don't happen in Glendarroch," was all Grace could say.

"These aren't Glendarroch folk, Mother," said Dougal. "They'll be bringing their wild southern ways here with them." He turned back to Brian. "Do *you* think he's been kidnapped?" he asked.

Brian frowned for a moment.

"I thought she was havering at first," he said slowly. "But the lassie knows the man Davenport and she thinks it's possible. And —" he glanced at his watch "— Harry hasn't been seen now for over three hours, and he has a concert to do in less than six. So where is he?"

Dougal nodded slowly. In a rather nasty way it made sense.

"So what do you want me to do?" he asked.

"What we've got to do, because it's the only thing we *can* do, is trace a brown Rolls Royce. That's what Charlie Davenport's got, and Bob saw Harry getting into it with him at the Town Hall. So it's safe to assume that wherever the Rolls Royce is, Harry won't be far away."

"Man, but that's useless! Look at the area we'll have to search. It's hundreds of square miles, and every minute the thing could be getting further away."

"I don't think so," said Brian. "Charlie Davenport's just holding Harry overnight so that he can't do this concert. Then he'll return him to Letir-Falloch safe and sound. So he's not going to take him far away, is he?"

"All the same, it's like looking for a needle in a haystack. Worse. At least a needle stays still."

"I know. It's not going to be easy. I'm off to Glendarroch now and then on to Letir-Falloch to see if anyone's seen any sign of it there. One thing. A brown Rolls Royce is gey kenspeckle. Someone must have noticed it somewhere."

"Aye. Maybe."

"And if you could get round the Ardvain folk, ask them."

"You think he might have been brought up here?"

"It's not likely, but it's possible. See what you can do."

"Just a minute. You say you think this man with the name like a sofa will be keeping a grip on Harry Shaw overnight?"

"That's right."

"Then he's got to have some shelter, hasn't he? A house, a hotel, maybe a but and ben somewhere."

"That's true, Dougal."

"Well, that narrows it a bit. But not much. All right. There's no point in hanging around. I'll follow you, and go up to the head of the glen if you go down to the village. Mind you, the man might have gone to the other side of Auchtarne. He might be halfway back to London by now. Or even Glasgow."

"He might, but there are others making enquiries in that direction. If they've left the area we'll get to know."

"Aye, but when?"

"That's the trouble. Probably too late."

"Right, then. Mother."

"Aye?" said Grace.

"I'll maybe be a wee thing late for my tea," said Dougal as he followed Brian out of the croft house and headed for his Land Rover.

At the top of the track Brian turned right to go down the hill to Glendarroch, and Dougal turned left, heading towards the top of the glen where the land narrowed and the mountains crowded in on both sides. He stopped at each croft on the way. Morag and Jamie Stewart had seen nothing, and by the time Dougal had been to the MacNeill croft and beyond that right to the head of the glen where the Moncur brothers lived silent and lonely lives, he was pretty sure that the brown Rolls Royce had not ventured in their direction. In these isolated areas anything that moved would have been instantly spotted by someone.

Heading down again he turned off to Inverdarroch, but the house was empty and he knew that Inverdarroch himself would be cutting his hay. He lurched along the track until he heard through the open Land Rover window the rattle of Inverdarroch's tractor and he stopped at the gate into the field and got out. Inverdarroch was driving placidly backwards and forwards,

the field almost finished. He caught sight of Dougal
striding towards him and he stopped and switched off
the tractor engine.

"Dougal," he said.

"Inverdarroch. Listen. Have you seen a brown Rolls
Royce today?"

"Aye," said Inverdarroch.

Dougal nodded as though that were what he had
expected and was turning away when he realised just
what Inverdarroch had said.

"You *have*?" he asked.

"I said so, didn't I?"

"Have you been cutting here all day?"

"Aye."

"So where did you see it?"

"It was on the track there. Heading towards Cragganmore Lodge."

Dougal thought for a minute. That confirmed what he
had said — that this Davenport would need somewhere
as shelter overnight, but he would never have thought
of Cragganmore. Why, no one had been near the place
for donkey's years.

"You're sure?"

"You don't seen brown Rolls Royces every day in life,"
said Inverdarroch. "Aye, I'm sure."

"When was this?"

Inverdarroch thought for a moment.

"I'd just eaten my piece, so it would have been around
eleven o'clock this morning."

That fitted with the times Brian had given Dougal.

"Fine."

"Then I saw it again just after two. Coming down
again."

Dougal looked puzzled.

"Coming down again?" he echoed.

"Aye. And they must have left someone up there."

"How do you make that out?"

"When the car went up there were three people in it.
When it came down there were only two. A shover and a
man sitting in the back."

Dougal stared at him in awe.

"Inverdarroch, you're fair astonishing!" he said

involuntarily.

Inverdarroch looked pleased.

"I never thought I'd live to hear you say that, Dougal," he said. "It means a lot to me. Eh — what have I done?"

"Come on. There's no time to lose. We've got to get Brian while he's still at Glendarroch. I'll give you a lift down."

"But my hay —"

"Never mind your hay. This is important."

"But the weather —"

"Stop girning, man! There's just a touch of mist coming in, it's no worse than that. Come on. It may be a matter of life and death."

Inverdarroch's jaw dropped and he stared at Dougal in amazement, but the thought of life and death spurred him into activity so he fell into step beside him and they made their way back across the newly cut field to the gate and Dougal's Land Rover.

9

Harry returned to the window and looked at it more closely than he had done before. There were two rows of three panes to the lower frame and two rows of three panes to the upper. Through the glass he could see that the putty holding the panes in place on the outside was cracked and broken through lack of paint and years of weathering. The room faced west so it would have its fair share of sunshine in the summer and driving wind, rain and snow in the winter. The fabric must be pretty far through, no matter how well built originally.

He still had the screwdriver in his pocket. He remembered having it in his hand when he came to meet Charlie in the Town Hall and how he had absent-mindedly put it in his pocket then and had forgotten about it since. He pulled it out and gently inserted it into the bottom left edge of the frame between the woodwork and the glass pane. He began to work his way round the pane, gently easing it outwards with the screwdriver as he did so.

In ten minutes he had reached his starting point again

and several times he had seen some of the hard, cracked putty fall away from the outside and drop on to the canopy just below. He hadn't heard it fall, but he remembered how he hadn't heard anything of Charlie leaving either, and he wondered if it were making a noise as it landed on the canopy and rolled across the glass and dropped into the drive. There was nothing he could do about it except pray that it wasn't heard. Anyway, one of the Bouncers, he was sure, was downstairs in the kitchen premises, and from the sound of the door opening and the creaking bedsprings, the other was probably in a room opposite his, and facing towards the back of the house.

He paused in his work and looked out of the window. The edge of his field of vision had crept in amazingly quickly. He could now barely see across to the far side of the drive outside, and he felt a surge of hope. If visibility dropped further it would make an escape from here easier.

He glanced at his watch and what he saw made him redouble his efforts. It was after two o'clock. Just over five hours to concert time and there was a lot to be got through before then. Sally had said he should rest. What a hope!

He gently thumped the loosened pane of glass in one corner and it pivoted outwards. He managed to grab one of the incoming corners before the pane could drop on to the canopy from whence it would have slid down and shattered on the ground below. To allow that to happen would really be pressing his luck too far. Then, turning the pane slightly, he drew it into the room. A cold draught swirled in, bringing the first of the mist with it.

He had made a hole to the outside world less than one foot by one foot, far too narrow to climb through, but it was a start.

Fifteen minutes later he removed the neighbouring centre bottom pane in the same way. It had been easier because this time he could reach his hand through the gap he had made, and with the screwdriver he had been able to chip away the rotten putty direct. But now came the crunch. He carefully examined the astragal between the two missing panels and he breathed a sigh of relief.

Like the putty, the wood of the frame itself had suffered through age and neglect. The astragal was rotten. He gave it a thump with the edge of his hand and it cracked and splintered with what seemed to him to be an ear-shattering noise. He stopped still and held his breath but there was no sound of movement from outside the room so perhaps the noise hadn't been as great as he had thought.

Then he began to work on the top left-hand pane. Soon it and the top centre pane joined the other two inside the room, carefully stacked against the skirting board, and he began to work at the wooden astragals. It wasn't difficult to crack them, but it was extremely difficult to do it quietly, and several times he found himself breathing heavily, not from exertion but in an effort to drown the noise he was making. He forced himself to stop. It wouldn't much matter whether the Bouncer outside thought he was escaping or having a heart attack: if the man decided to investigate now, he was finished.

At last it was done and he stood for a while, listening. The house seemed as shrouded in silence as it was in the mist which was snaking into the room in eager swirls, wrapping clammy hands round him, and he shivered involuntarily.

He managed to ease his way through the hole he had made in the frame. For a ghastly minute he thought he wasn't going to be able to get his shoulders through and would have to hang there until he was found and dragged back in again, but a desperate wriggle freed him and he landed on the glass of the canopy directly over one of the points where a metal bracket sprang from the wall to carry the glass roof.

He felt his stomach curl as he put his weight on it. It hadn't looked terribly sturdy when he had seen it outside, but although it seemed to sway and tremble alarmingly, it held. The slope downwards was gentle and he managed to dig his toes into the rone, feeling the gathered moss from years of neglect give against his shoe.

After a bit of scrabbling which seemed to echo round the house with the decibels of a pipe band he swung himself over the edge of the canopy, his hands grasping the guttering, hanging in space and frightened to drop, not quite sure how far there was to go to the ground.

But the decision was made for him. There was a rending sound and a section of the guttering gave way. He dropped about four feet and jarred his legs because he thought it would have been much further. He had the presence of mind to hang on to the piece of guttering which had come away in his hand so it didn't drop to the ground with an enormous clatter, and he laid it carefully down at the side of the front door before slipping away from the house into the gathering mist. When, after twenty yards, he glanced back, he found the house had disappeared as though it had never been there.

10

The mist grew thicker as they climbed higher. Mr MacPherson sat in the front of the Land Rover beside Dougal and peered uneasily through the windscreen. At first, on the lower ground, there had just been a general haziness which had been gradually creeping over the land during the latter part of the morning, but now that haziness had thickened, visibility had dropped and great swathes of the mist seemed to blow into the windscreen and divide to let the Land Rover through.

The track kept unwinding about twenty yards ahead of them. Beyond that everything was lost. Dougal had tried putting on the headlights but it only had the effect of throwing the light back at them from the mist and he had soon switched them off again.

He wondered whether he was doing the right thing. But Brian had convinced him, and certainly if Harry Shaw were being kept up here at Cragganmore Lodge against his will, and if the police had been reluctant to make a move, then the least he could do was to lend support towards his release.

Behind him Bob and Inverdarroch were huddled on the rear seats as the Land Rover lurched and bounced up the uneven surface of the track towards the lodge.

Through the rear window he could occasionally see

the looming shape of the Blairs' van following them. In that, he knew, Brian was driving, and Eddie was in the passenger seat and an unhappy Archie Menzies was sitting in the back. Brian had gathered seven of them. He had said that the more they had the less likely it was that there would be any physical trouble.

"And having you there, Minister, should make it even less likely."

"I sincerely trust you are right, Brian," Mr MacPherson had said, wondering if it came to a rough-house of some kind how much of a liability he would be himself.

"I'm sure I am. Besides, it'll put them on the wrong foot. They'll not exactly expect to see a minister standing on their doorstep."

"I daresay. But how many of these people are there?"

"We've no idea. According to Inverdarroch Harry must have been left up there by this man Davenport, but we can be pretty certain that he wouldn't be left there alone. We just don't know how many others there may be."

It was all rather worrying, and glancing sideways at Dougal's grim face Mr MacPherson realised that he was worried too, though perhaps the grimness was caused by the lessening visibility, which seemed worse at every tortuous turn the track took and every foot they gained in height.

Suddenly the track widened and a shapeless shadow seemed to loom out of the mist ahead of them. Dougal put his foot on the brake and the Land Rover stopped.

"We're here," he said, and he switched off the engine and opened the driver's door.

They got out and stood for a moment waiting for the van to join them. It drifted quietly out of the mist and came to a halt alongside the Land Rover.

Brian, when he emerged, was crisp and fast.

"Right," he said. "Bob, Eddie. Round the back in case they try to get out with him. I don't suppose they will, but we can't take any risks. Not in these conditions. They may have a car there. Make sure they can't get it out quickly. We'll give you two minutes to get there."

Bob and Eddie disappeared and Brian glanced at his

watch.

Mr MacPherson found his ears straining, but he could hear nothing. The world was absolutely still. Not a breath of wind anywhere. Not a sound except the slight scuff of a foot on the weed-covered gravel of the drive.

"Right," said Brian. "On you go, Minister."

Mr MacPherson swallowed uncomfortably and led the way forward. The frontage of the lodge loomed out of the mist and he made his way along it till he came to the front door.

It was big and solid but the paint was peeling so badly that the bare boards showed through in places. There was an ancient bell-pull beside it and after taking a deep breath he pulled it.

There was silence inside the house, and he wasn't sure whether that was because the bell rang so distantly that they couldn't hear it from here, or whether it hadn't rung at all. Looking at the condition of the house it was probably the latter.

They waited and nothing happened. Then Brian stepped forward and hammered at the door with his fist, and the noise was sudden enough to waken the dead.

It echoed into silence and the mist seemed to wrap itself more thickly round them. There was no sound from inside the house.

Archie appeared out of the mist.

"There are folk in there," he said in a hoarse whisper. "Or there have been. There's a Calor gas heater in that drawing room and it's on."

"Right," said Brian. "Feet. Okay?"

Mr MacPherson stifled a protest as Brian stepped back and put his foot to the front door.

"Don't worry, Minister. If we cause any damage we'll make it good."

He kicked again and Eddie put his shoulder to it and the noise echoed dreadfully after the former silence.

"Come on," shouted Brian suddenly. "Open up or we'll break the door down. There are people at the back as well."

He gave the door another kick and there was an ominous crack from the woodwork.

"I'm not quite sure how the law would react to this,"

said Mr MacPherson.

Brian grinned suddenly.

"It's all right, Minister," he said. "No harm done. We've woken them up. Listen."

Sure enough they could hear bolts being drawn on the other side of the door and a moment later it opened and a face looked suspiciously out at them.

It was a fighter's face, but one which had gone to seed, thought Mr MacPherson hopefully. The eyes were small but startled at the moment and the chin was quite definitely blue.

"Wot's the idea?" the face began and then it registered Mr MacPherson and the jaw dropped at the sight of the dog collar. "Wot you doin' 'ere, Vicar?" he asked with a return to truculence.

"I am not a vicar," said Mr MacPherson mildly. "I am a minister of the Church of Scotland, and I should be grateful for a few words with Mr Harry Shaw."

"Mr 'Oo?"

"Come on," said Brian. "We know he's here. And there are plenty of us all round the house. Harry has a prior engagement this evening. With us."

"Dunno wot you're talkin' about," said the face.

"Then you won't mind if we come in and look for him."

"Listen, me and me mate, we're 'ere on maintenance—"

Brian stepped forward and the man tried to close the door but Brian's foot was in the gap. The man looked from one to the other. Mr MacPherson noticed that Inverdarroch had picked up a length of old guttering from somewhere and was beating it speculatively into the palm of his left hand. He felt himself being pushed gently to one side and saw Archie leaning against the door, gradually increasing the weight he was putting on it, and the man inside found it more and more difficult to keep it partially closed. As Brian lent his weight too the door gradually swung open.

"'Ere, wot you think you're doin'?" demanded the man who was now fully revealed as a muscularly flabby character of medium height in his stocking soles. The latter fact gave Mr MacPherson a great deal of comfort. He had a feeling that people did not get dangerously pugnacious when they weren't properly shod.

Somehow he found himself inside the hall with the other three in front of him, and the man retreating before them. Inverdarroch had left his guttering outside but Archie had found a stout walking stick in a stand just inside the front door. Another man appeared at the top of the stairs and when they caught sight of him, Inverdarroch turned back to the door, went out and a moment later a piercing whistle rent the air. Then Inverdarroch returned to be followed a minute later by Eddie and Bob.

The sight of yet more visitors seemed to knock the stuffing out of the two men and Mr MacPherson saw a look pass between them before their shoulders sagged.

"Where is he?" demanded Brian.

There was silence for a moment, and then the man on the stairs stood aside and the movement showed Mr MacPherson where Harry Shaw must be. Brian herded both men before him as they climbed the stairs to the landing and watched as one of them produced a key and unlocked a door. He pushed it open and stood sullenly aside.

"Right, Harry," said Brian, walking into the room ahead of them. "Everything's under control — God!"

The exclamation silence them all as they crowded into the room behind him.

It was empty and chilly, and the mist swirled through the gap in the window.

Brian strode across to it and glanced out.

"He's gone," he said, and he turned back and looked balefully at the two men who had followed them all in.

"'E can't be off," said one of them incredulously.

"Well, he has. Look for yourself. No one here. He got out by the window."

"Wait a minute," said Archie. "If he's escaped, why didn't we pass him on the track on our way up? That's the only way out of here."

"Because he isn't on it," said Brian. "He's lost the track in the mist. He's out there somewhere on the moor. Alone. Now we really do have trouble."

Chapter Six

1

The ridges and stones and tussocks of weeds on the track were the only solid things in the world. All round him was a pall of greyness, impenetrable and wet. The mist swirled past him in damp streamers and there was nothing else. Not a sound. Not a breath of wind.

Charlie had said The Boys would see him back to Letir-Falloch in the morning and that implied that they had a car somewhere, for he was certain Charlie was on his way back to London now, not wanting to spend any more time than he had to in the backwoods. It was probably in one of the outhouses. He'd thought briefly of trying to find it and get away in it. But only briefly. Even in the unlikely event of the key being in the ignition, in these damp conditions it might not have fired quickly enough. He wasn't going to risk recapture. No, he was better on his own feet. It might be long enough before The Boys found he was missing.

For the first time Harry wondered just how far he had to go. The track had seemed to wind on for ever when they had been on their way up in Charlie's Rolls Royce, but he knew they had been travelling very slowly. He wished he'd had a chance to check the milometer so that he had an idea of distance. Anything between two miles and four miles before he could expect any kind of help in the way of a lift.

And somewhere down there people would be gathering outside the Auchtarne Town Hall, queueing for admission to his concert. Apart from them there were the people who had helped him to set it up. And the roadies would have arrived by now with the P.A. system. And above all there was Sally. Funny to think that perhaps a week or so ago his inexplicable absence might not have worried her too much. But after all that had happened since he knew that she would be out of her mind by now, for a glance at his watch showed that the time was just after three o'clock. Four and a half hours to go . . .

Well, if he kept going steadily he could reach the road in perhaps an hour. One good thing which came out of this was that he was probably able to progress on foot just about as fast as the Rolls Royce had.

Suddenly he stopped.

Where was the track?

There was heather under his feet, not the ridges and weeds and stones he had become used to.

While his mind had been occupied with other things he must have inadvertently stepped off the track on to the moor and he hadn't noticed. He cursed his stupidity. The track was his lifeline and now he had lost it.

He stood stock still, heart thumping, and listened. There was no sound. Nothing to guide him. He was lost in a featureless grey blanket and had no idea which way he should go.

He began to cast around him in a widening circle, hoping that he might be lucky enough to touch the edge of the track again, but all that happened was that he became even more disorientated, so much so that he began to doubt whether he had in fact been travelling in a circle rather than a straight line, and that simply made matters worse.

His heart pounded faster, not with exertion but with fear, sheer blind panic at the thought that he was in the grip of elements so much more powerful than himself and he had to force it down with great determination to prevent it from getting the better of him and leave him screaming and sobbing for help in the middle of the moor miles from anywhere and anyone.

Think. Think. Think . . .

Well, whatever the visibility, which couldn't have been more than ten yards, he could detect the slope of the hill they were on. It wasn't much to go on, but if he followed it he should make progress roughly in a straight line, and from the view from his prison window before the mist closed in completely he knew that the downward slope would take him away from the house and not have him blundering into it again unexpectedly.

But progress was difficult. Perhaps with the realisation that he was no longer on the track his feet suddenly became entangled in tussocks of heather. He almost went his length when he dropped into an unexpected dip. He would have to slow his speed to avoid a broken or at least a twisted ankle, in spite of the instinct which was shouting at him to hurry, hurry, hurry.

Suddenly he stopped and listened. There was a sound in the air. At first it was simply a vague and indistinguishable murmur, but it grew and turned into the sound of car engines labouring up the slope of the track. More than one of them, he thought, but one would have been enough. He shouted and then realised the futility of that. With the noise of the engines no one was going to hear him. In any case it might not be wise. It could possibly be another supply of Bouncers come to take over the back shift. But if that were so they wouldn't be using two cars. It was more likely that they were friends. Perhaps a lot of them.

Frantically he tried to decide which direction the noise was coming from and how far away it might be but it was impossible. At one moment the sound seemed to be almost at his elbow, the next perhaps half a mile away across the bleak expanse of moorland. The noise itself was moving, of course, and that made it more difficult, and there seemed to be some kind of an echo effect which made it seem to be coming from two different directions at the same time. He wasn't even sure now whether he was hearing one engine or two. He set off one way and then decided that the noise was diminishing rather than growing, so he turned and headed in the opposite direction only to find that it was diminishing that way as well.

And within a couple of minutes the noise had faded into silence, his chance of human contact had gone, and he was left alone again with the mist creeping insidiously around him and beading his hair with moisture.

2

They kept talking and shouting. It didn't matter what they said, just so long as you could keep in touch with the man next to you in the line.

The mist was so thick that Dougal, who at first had cursed Harry for being so stupid as to wander off the track, had to acknowledge that it would have been a very easy thing to do, especially someone from the city who didn't know about country ways. And, he added charitably to himself, it wasn't exactly the youngster's fault. He couldn't help being kidnapped by thugs and carried off to a place the like of Cragganmore Lodge. He might have been daft on the loch last week, but this was no fault of his own.

There was nothing more certain than that Harry must have veered off the track. But where? How far down had he been when he lost it? And furthermore, had he veered off it to left or to right?

Dougal thought that if he had gone left he would very quickly have realised his mistake and ought to have been able to find his way back reasonably easily, for the lower slopes of Ben Darroch started to rise very steeply only a hundred yards or so from the track itself, and the man would have found himself climbing and known, if he had any sense at all — a matter which Dougal was not sure about — that he was wrong. So the Mountain Rescue team, when they arrived, had agreed that their efforts should be concentrated on the right-hand side of the track where the downward slope was more gentle but would have led him back towards civilisation.

Another thing about the calling, of course, was that with any luck Harry Shaw might hear them. That is, if anything had happened to him, like turning an ankle or falling into a gully. But Dougal remembered the time he had fallen into Poacher's Drop and knocked himself out and had missed the search because he had not been conscious to hear it. There was always the chance that something similar had happened here.

He kept talking, talking nonsense, while all these thoughts marched through his mind. To his left was a man from Auchtarne who had worked at Cragganmore in the shooting season as a beater for thirty-five years in succession except for the war, he'd told Dougal, an old man now but wiry and strong and who knew the moors like the back of his hand. And to his right was one of the thugs from Cragganmore Lodge itself. Once they had found Harry gone their resistance had crumbled. They clearly lived in mortal terror of what Charlie Davenport would say when he heard they had let Harry escape and, what was worse, put his life in danger, and they were only too anxious to co-operate, do anything to help find the man again even, thought Dougal with some amusement, to the extent of taking part in the search although they were equipped neither by training nor inclination for the job as he realised when he listened to the man on his right. His talking consisted of a strange mixture of swearing at the conditions and praying for his own personal safety, often cut off in mid-phrase as the man took a tumble in the heather, and then resumed with greater feeling as he pulled himself to his feet again and Dougal wondered whether in fact it might not have been silly to bring the pair of them. It had seemed a good idea when they set off. The more they had on the search the wider they could spread the line and so have more chance of success, and rather than leave the men at Cragganmore with at least one police officer when they couldn't spare one, it was better to have the thugs along with them. One thing was certain. They were so scared of these alien surroundings that the last thing they would think of was trying to escape.

Along the line he heard the voices of men unseen. If it hadn't been for the voices he might have been alone on the hill, for he could see nothing of those on either side of him, except occasionally when the looming figure of the thug veered too close and out of position and had to be directed back again.

Every now and then they stopped to listen but there was no sound other than their own voices hallooing across the emptiness of the moor.

Of course, Dougal reckoned that by the time they had alerted the Mountain Rescue team and got them to Cragganmore Lodge and organised the search Harry Shaw must be at least an hour ahead of them, and by this time he could be anywhere and, unfortunately, in any condition.

3

Taking the downward slope was all very well, but every now and then the downward slope began to move upward again and he had to veer to one side to find where it continued down. Perhaps, of course, it was simply that he wasn't walking straight, and there was no doubt that he hadn't the remotest idea where he was heading now. Not that he'd had very much from the moment he had realised he'd left the track. All sense of direction had long since gone, except for up and down. He still knew that the sky was above him and the ground underneath and the fact that he had to cling so firmly and consciously to that idea was a matter for some concern.

And then without warning the slope became almost a drop. His foot went down much further than he had expected it to, and he was thrown forward with the suddenness of it. The next foot went down to save himself and it went even further and then his balance was gone and his feet went from under him and with a shout of dismay he found himself rolling down the heathery slope and wondering if and when he would stop.

It seemed to go on for ever, and he wished he hadn't told himself that he still knew the difference between up and down, because he certainly didn't any longer, and after what seemed an endless time he fetched up with a thump at the bottom of the slope, lying in a thin trickle of water which must have been a burn when the weather was less dry, and he found himself lying there looking up at where the sky should be, all the breath knocked out of his body and wondering fearfully what damage had been done.

Very cautiously he tested his arms and his neck. Everything moved all right and there was no pain, so he tried his legs and breathed a heartfelt sigh of relief. No pain there either. Nothing was broken. Not even sprained. He had been very lucky. Possibly the springi-ness of the heather had cushioned most of the bumps on the way down.

He picked himself up and looked round, but there

wasn't much point in doing that. It didn't help. There was nothing to see.

The thin trickle of water in the gully into which he had fallen was the only sign of movement, and he began to pick his way carefully up the steep slope down which he had fallen and eventually arrived at the top on hands and knees, panting hard, soaked to the skin and with a tear in the left knee of his jeans. There was a trickle of blood just below his knee where he must have scraped a stone. It looked black in the greyness around him.

He had been lucky. Very lucky. And he sat at the top of the slope, shivering, not with cold, for it wasn't cold, but with reaction, and scared to move any further in case it happened again and he might have used up his share of luck for one day.

4

There can't have been such activity at Cragganmore Lodge for very many years. The front door stood open. There were cars and vans and Land Rovers parked on the forecourt. There was a constant murmur from the walkie-talkie in Sergeant Murray's police car as the searchers were directed by radio and sent in their reports. So far they had found nothing.

Dr Wallace remembered the last time he had been up here. It must have been ten years ago. No, more. He smiled at the memory. Some old buffer in a shooting party had tripped over his gun and peppered a colleague in a tender spot with shotgun pellets and he had had to come and administer comfort and relief to a very irate elderly gentleman with iron-grey hair and a bristling iron-grey moustache who actually said "Damme, sir" at the start of every sentence, who had taken it as a personal affront that Wallace had had to come and treat him and who had roundly abused him while lying on his stomach on a sofa with his trousers down.

That day there had been a stir at Cragganmore almost as big as today's.

But this stir had been dead for an hour now. All that was left was the debris of human activity, the empty cars, plastic carrier bags in which ordinary shoes had been left in exchange for stout boots. And there were a few human remains, too, he thought. Himself for one. Sergeant Murray in the police car for another. And Ian MacPherson sitting in the Panda with Sally Shaw, trying to keep her mind from imagining the worst.

He had told her not to worry, tried to reassure her that at this time of the year the moor was a much kinder place than it was in winter, that the weather forecast had been that clearer weather was expected from the west during the afternoon, and that once the mist cleared they would find him. He didn't mention that with his lack of experience of the conditions Harry Shaw might well have broken an ankle, if not a leg, or if he had been particularly unlucky, a neck.

Her main concern had been that he hadn't eaten, that she had cooked him a good lunch which was now ruined and what could she do when they did find him because she hadn't the raw materials or the time to prepare another meal and she was sure he would be hungry.

Wallace stood at the edge of the forecourt and looked out across where the moor must be if he could see it, wondering what was happening out there. It wasn't cold, so there shouldn't be too much of a problem with exposure, but the mist was damp and clinging. One thing was that the light, such as it was, would last for hours yet. Not like a winter search when there was the frantic need for caution combined with haste to cover as much ground while they could see where they were and what they were doing and stood some chance of finding the victim for whom they were searching.

He walked over to the police car and glanced in at Sergeant Murray in the passenger seat.

"Nothing?" asked Wallace.

The Sergeant shook his head.

"No," he said. "No one's seen anything of him. Of course, he's an hour ahead of them, and at least they haven't found him with a broken leg. I blame myself for this, you know, Doctor. I should have paid more attention to Mrs Shaw."

"You can't blame yourself just because she was right. The whole thing sounds pretty bizarre to me."

"It is certainly that, but —"

"And even if you had taken action immediately you'd never have traced Harry Shaw up here on your own. Not in the time."

"That is true. Local knowledge is the most powerful weapon we have at our disposal," said the Sergeant sententiously, and Wallace hid a smile. Sergeant Murray was trying to justify his lack of action.

Suddenly he straightened up, alert. Murray noticed the movement and glanced at him.

"What is it?" he asked.

"I could swear I felt a breath of wind just then," muttered Wallace, keeping his voice low as though to speak louder would allow the wind to hear him and decide not to come back. And if the wind blew the mist might well disappear . . .

He felt something touch his cheek.

"It was," he said. "I think our luck's in, Murray."

Murray had climbed out of the car and felt the wind himself. Just the gentlest of movement, something they might well have missed had it not been so important to them.

"Aye, you're right," he said. "This'll clear it. We'll find him now."

"Mphm," Wallace agreed. "Just pray that he hasn't broken a leg."

5

Something touched Harry on the back of the neck very gently and he started to his feet in surprise and whirled round. There was no one there.

He stood listening, but heard nothing.

And then it came again, this time touching his face.

A breeze. The gentlest of breezes, and he felt relief. It was movement, action, something happening in the still silence all round him.

That was all it meant at first, nothing more than activity, but then he noticed that the mist all round him was beginning to writhe as though in pain. Swathes of it began to move, and it gradually came to him that this could be the end of his trouble, that the breeze was his saviour, that the mist would clear and that he would be able to see again.

Then there came a rustling as the wind blew stronger and stirred the stout heather stalks under his feet and the mist moved faster and began to lift.

He could see the ground for twenty yards round him now. Thirty. Forty.

His field of vision expanded more and more. He could see the gully into which he had fallen, though the mist still moved there in the depths and he couldn't see the bottom. On top it was clearing all the time.

It moved further and further away but nothing more came into view. Just more moorland spreading outwards from him as the mist blew silently away. Mile after mile of it rising to the mountains which very slowly began to loom visibly again.

He stared at it all in dismay. There was nothing there but empty moor and grey sky and the distant mountains.

He turned slowly, meeting the same scene as he went, until he had turned a hundred and eighty degrees and suddenly there, not a quarter of a mile away and just below him lay a house. It seemed so close that he thought that if he had shouted when he had climbed out of the gully they must have heard him.

One of the chimneys was smoking, and there was a collection of outbuildings, a tree grew in the backyard and the whole place looked infinitely desirable.

He began to stumble down the slope towards it as the mist lifted further and drifted steadily away. A glance at his watch told him that it was five o'clock.

6

"Dougal said he might be late for his tea," said Grace, "so you and me'll just have ours."

Morag turned from the kitchen window.

"Do you think they'll find him?" she asked.

"Och, aye," said Grace. "Now that the mist's lifted. So long as the lad hasn't gone stravaiging too far over the moor, but being city bred he'll not have done that. You set the table, lass."

"Don't bother about me, Mrs Lachlan. I'll need to get back and get my father's tea."

"Is he not out on the search?"

Morag shook her head.

"Not him," she said. "As soon as Dougal asked him he said he was having trouble with his tubes and wouldn't risk them out in the mist."

"Bad, are they?"

"They got bad just as he said it and they cleared up as soon as Dougal had gone."

A shadow passed the window and Grace looked out but it had disappeared before she could see who it was. The door opened and a stranger staggered into the room.

"Mercy on us —!" said Grace and she hurried forward because the man seemed on the brink of falling. "Here — come and sit down," she said, leading him to Dougal's chair beside the fire. "Gracious, you're soaking, laddie! Bide you here and I'll get you some dry things of Dougal's —"

"Mrs Lachlan — it's him!" said Morag in an awestruck voice.

"It's who, lass?"

"It's *Vincent*. The man they're all out looking for."

"Do you tell me?" said Grace, unimpressed. "Well, if it is he's a wet Vincent and he'd be better out of those things straightaway. Fancy going out in clothes like that. And see those shoes! Nothing but cardboard and string!"

She bustled away into Dougal's bedroom, leaving Morag goggle-eyed at having this celebrity suddenly in the same room with her. Not that he looked like a celebrity now. He was tired and dirty and blood had oozed from a cut below his left knee. He didn't look like the authoritative personality she had seen in the magazine photographs. He looked just like what he was — a young man who'd been lost for more than three hours on the moor in the mist. The surprising thing was that he'd survived it so well.

Grace returned with a dry set of clothes.

"Now you get out of those wet things," she commanded. "Can you manage by yourself?"

The man nodded.

"I've been doing it for years," he said.

"Good for you. There's a dry towel. I don't expect the things'll fit awful well, but they'll do. I'll get something hot for you. It's nearly ready anyway."

She and Morag returned to the cooker and the sink, diplomatically turning their heads as he undressed, towelled himself vigorously and then dressed again.

"I'd better go and tell them he's safe," said Morag. "Otherwise they'll be out there for hours yet."

"All right, lass. You have your Land Rover?"

"Aye."

"Come back when you can and we'll have a talk about it all, eh?" said Grace. "There hasn't been excitement like this at Ardvain for many a long day."

Morag nodded and left and a moment later Grace heard the engine of the Land Rover start and recede as Morag drove away up the track to the road.

Grace surveyed the new arrival again. As she had suggested the clothes were not exactly a good fit. Vincent seemed to be lost in them, because he was a lot smaller than Dougal, and she smiled. After a moment he smiled back at her.

"D'you think I'll do for Ascot?" he asked.

She felt relief. There could be little wrong with the man if he could see the humour in the situation.

"How do you feel?" she asked.

"Better now," he said. "Listen, I've been walking across the moor and I got lost. How quickly can I get to Auchtarne from here?"

"Never you heed about that, lad. There have been folk out looking for you, and Morag's just gone to have the search called off."

"But I've got to be in Auchtarne —"

"Aye, aye, this concert of yours. I've heard about that. You'll be there in plenty of time. If you feel you can do it, that is."

"Course I can do it. And I'm going to do it. Here, you've no idea what a relief it is to hear you say that — about being able to get there in time."

"Hungry?" she asked.

He thought about it for a moment and then grinned

again.

"I think I could eat a horse," he said and a frown suddenly crossed his face. "That's what Charlie said ... Anyway, if you haven't got a horse a sheep would do."

"You'll get a good plate of cockaleekie —"

"Cockaleekie?" His eyes brightened. "I haven't had cockaleekie since I can't remember when."

"Well, you'll get it now. And after that there's a gigot and potatoes and peas, and Dougal aye likes a steamie pudding when he's been out on the moor so there's a spotted dog —"

And when the time came Harry ate the lot.

7

Dr Wallace wasn't quite sure why he chose to drive home by way of the Town Hall. Sheer vulgar curiosity, he supposed, but there had been a couple of calls waiting for him when he got home and he'd done them and since he'd finished the last one at just about half-past seven it seemed a good opportunity to see what was happening here.

He'd had a look at Harry Shaw at the Lachlan croft and found nothing wrong with him. The lad had had a fright and he'd be stiff by the morning, but he'd insisted that he was going to do the concert and Wallace had seen no reason to try to dissuade him.

He drew up opposite the Town Hall. The lights were on inside but the audience were clearly all in and even as he stopped he heard the ear-splitting shriek of joyful young voices which must announce that Vincent had just stepped on to the stage.

So that was all right, he thought. He prepared to slip the car into gear and drive off home when he was startled by the passenger door opening and someone slipped into the seat beside him.

"Good evening, Sandy," said Ian MacPherson.

"You're not in there shrieking with the rest of them?" asked Wallace.

"I feel it better to leave the pleasures of the young to the young."

"Coward."

"On this occasion I accept the rebuke. Anyway, I couldn't get a seat. Mind you, I didn't try very hard."

They listened as the screaming rose to a fever pitch.

"There hasn't been a noise like that in there since Mafeking was relieved," said the minister.

"Is that so? Personally I don't remember that."

"The hall is packed, I'm told."

"It certainly sounds it."

"They've even opened up the gallery and that hasn't happened since the Auchtarne Gilbert and Sullivan Society last did *The Mikado*."

"I hope it holds up."

Out of the shrieking hysteria within the hall came the sudden thrum of a guitar, amplified enormously, sending the whole Town Hall vibrating. Wallace listened to it for a moment.

"The volume seems right here. I shudder to think what it must be like in there," he said. "Still, I'm glad he made it. For the lifeboat's sake. And there would have been a great many disappointed customers otherwise."

"I believe the folk setting up the equipment have done a marvellous job, considering Harry Shaw has been *hors de combat* all afternoon. Of course, they have worked with him before so I presume it was all fairly routine."

The pounding rhythm throbbed out of the building.

"Oh, well," said Wallace philosophically, "the surgery will be packed on Monday due to a mysterious epidemic of deafness. However, it's all in a good cause."

"Indeed. I'm told Harry Shaw has raised nearly fifteen hundred pounds for the lifeboat fund."

Wallace pursed his lips in a silent whistle.

"Almost worth a few burst eardrums, eh?" he said.

They sat for a while as the sun sank behind the buildings and the Town Hall vibrated with the sound of the guitar and Harry Shaw's voice, unrecognisable through the amplification, asked the audience *What Will You Do To Me Next?*

8

The old man was crouched over the central mound like a

very tall garden gnome at the edge of a fish pond. He was
so intent on what he was doing that he wasn't aware of
anyone near him until Harry's shadow fell over him and
he said "Hi."

Then he started and unwound himself and stood
stooping and towering over him, a trowel in his hand,
and his floppy off-white hat shading his face from the
strong sunlight which poured down from overhead.

"Mr Shaw," said Mr MacAulay. "Very good to see you,
sir. I understand your concert was a rousing success."

"Aye, it was, Mr MacAulay, and I feel a lot better for
getting it over."

"I was sorry to miss it, sir."

Harry grinned at him.

"Were you?" he asked. "Be honest."

MacAulay smiled back, a slightly sad smile, he
thought.

"Well, to tell you the truth, I don't think it was — what
is the expression? — exactly my scene. But I understand
you did not require my presence in any case. The hall
was full."

"It was packed. By the end you couldn't breathe."
Harry took a deep breath, relishing the cleanness of
the air compared with the memory of the Town Hall
two nights ago. "You finding interesting things?" he
asked.

"Mr Shaw, you find me in the process of kicking
myself."

"Oh? What are you doing that for?"

"I fear I have let my enthusiasm run away with me."

He turned and looked down at the central mound, his
whole attitude crestfallen and disappointed. Harry felt
an unaccountable sympathy for him.

"You mean there's nothing there?" he said. MacAulay
shook his head. "No treasure chest? No hidden gold?"

"I fear not, sir. This mound simply covers a large
boulder which is perfectly and boringly natural."

Harry felt an acute sense of disappointment, not
because of the lack of archaeological treasures, but for
the man who stood so despondently in front of him.

"I have been misled," said MacAulay. "No. That's not
quite true. I have misled myself. No one else has been

responsible for it. Professor Stewart Thomson's original article simple implied that he felt there might be an interesting site here. I think possibly my family's connections with Letir-Falloch have led me to believe there would be more here than there is. I feel too that I have misled Mr Gillies. I must ring and tell him that the deal's off. There are the remains of a stone circle, sir. Of that there is no doubt, but in itself it is a very minor affair. Why, there isn't even a single stone left standing. I have expected too much."

"I'm sorry to hear that."

"So am I, sir. So am I."

They stood silently in the sunshine for a while, listening to the distant rooks cawing in the elms.

"So there was no reason why the concert shouldn't have taken place here after all."

"None. I have made something of a fool of myself, sir."

"If you have, then I've done the same. Coming here, getting myself half-drowned, having the Mountain Rescue people called out after me."

"I understand the latter was hardly your fault, Mr Shaw."

"True, but it wouldn't have happened if I'd never come here."

"And the lifeboat wouldn't have benefited by your generosity."

"Well, there is that, I suppose. And I've found Sally again . . ."

"I beg your pardon?"

"Nothing. And you've found your old home again."

"That's true. And I've rid myself of a dream. I don't want it. And I've solved the riddle of the stone circle."

"So, maybe we *have* made fools of ourselves, Mr MacAulay, but it hasn't all been a waste of time, has it?"

Mr MacAulay looked at him for a long time and then nodded, a slow smile breaking out across his face.

"I guess that's very true, sir," he said.

"Will you be coming back?"

"I think not. Not now. There is nothing to come back for."

Harry nodded.

"No. That's right. I don't think I'll be coming back

either," he said.

9

"You'd have been quicker driving to Auchtarne if you're catching the train south," said Eddie.

He glanced round at the pair of them sitting behind him in the ferry.

"I know," said Harry. "We could have taken the car to Glasgow and flown to London, too."

As they cleared the headland Eddie turned the ferry and set course for Auchtarne. Behind them Glendarroch fell away, the low sunlight shimmering on the water and the little houses lying still in the breathless heat of a perfect summer morning.

"So what's the idea?" he asked.

"Sentiment," said Harry.

Eddie glanced at him in surprise and he heard Sally giggle beside him.

"Really?" he asked.

"Well, no, not really. Partly. I love the loch, in spite of what it did to me. But going this way and catching the train from Auchtarne, Charlie Davenport can't get at me."

"You trying to avoid him again?"

Harry grinned.

"Yes. I should be in his office in —" he glanced at his watch "— an hour's time. Nine o'clock. To sign the great new contract."

Eddie whistled.

"You're cutting it fine."

"Aye. Something tells me I'll not make it."

There was silence for a while.

"Why don't you have him up for kidnap?" Eddie asked.

"No fun in that," said Harry. "That's why I've asked everyone not to say anything to the police, so that they've nothing to report to the procurator fiscal."

Eddie grinned.

"Sergeant Murray doesn't know if he's on his head or his heels," he said. "First Sally asks him to get you back because you've been kidnapped and he doesn't do anything about it. And then when he finds you *have* been kidnapped you both tell him you weren't. The poor man's confused."

"I know. But I've got a better way to deal with Charlie. More personal. At the moment I'm enjoying thinking about him getting frantic on the telephone trying to find out where I am. Taking the ferry and getting the train from Auchtarne to Glasgow means that I'm out of contact for at least five hours. That's long enough to make him sweat. Serve him right."

"But what about the contract? It's a big one, isn't it?" Harry nodded.

"Nearly as big as the American one," he said. "I'm not going to sign it."

"What?" Eddie almost yelped.

"No. I've had enough. Enough of Charlie Davenport. Enough of being screamed at. Enough of jet-setting round the world. I just want an ordinary life like an ordinary bloke. Well, it won't be all that ordinary, because I've made a lot of money, much more than an ordinary bloke makes in a lifetime."

"So what are you going to do?"

"I'm opting out."

Eddie glanced round again in amazement and saw them sitting close together on the thwart, arms round each other, and Sally was smiling happily.

"I got worried when he was enjoying setting up that concert on Saturday," she said. "I thought this is giving him the taste for it again, and I didn't really want that to happen."

"You never said, Chicken," said Harry.

"Well, you're such a thrawn devil. If I'd said anything you'd have said you *had* got the taste for it again and you'd have gone ahead."

"That was sly."

"I know. Wasn't it?"

"But I got enthusiastic about the Saturday concert because it was different. It had some sort of purpose, and somehow it made the rest of the business seem unreal. And after what Charlie did, I thought I don't want any part of a business which can treat people this way."

"So what are you going to do?" asked Eddie. "Settle at

Letir-Falloch and become a gentleman of leisure?"

"Not on your nellie. Funny, you know. That bloke MacAulay and me. We've both failed in a way. But in another way we've succeeded. He's laid a couple of ghosts. His stone circle's nothing like as marvellous as it was in his imagination. And he doesn't feel he wants to belong to Letir-Falloch anymore. Me, I've caused nothing but trouble since I got here, but at least I've done something for the lifeboat."

"You have that," said Eddie.

"And what's more important, I've found Sally again." Eddie saw him draw her tightly to him. "And I know what I'm going to do now. I'm not coming back to Letir-Falloch. Might sell the place. I don't know. Haven't thought as far ahead as that yet. Probably wouldn't be easy to sell anyway, seeing it was so easy to buy. No, first thing is to use some of my money to buy an electrician's business in Glasgow. I've found a couple up for sale, and that's what we're going to have a look at now."

He turned and stared absently at the view of the hills rising on all sides, grey and purple in the early morning sun, and the polished bronze of the loch itself, flat and calm except where the wake of the ferry creamed and spread out behind them and disappeared into the distance.

"I think I may miss all this," he said. "It's fantastic. And it's done me a lot of good healthwise. And it's helped me to see things more clearly. But it's lonely. Too little happening for me. I found that on the moor the other day. So I'm going back to where I belong." Eddie saw him squeeze Sally's waist and she laid her head on his shoulder. "Where we both belong. And after that," he said grinning up at Eddie, the dark eyes relaxed and at peace, "we're going to live happily ever after."

If you have enjoyed this book, see overleaf for details of others in the *TAKE THE HIGH ROAD* series.

TAKE THE HIGH ROAD

SUMMER'S GLOAMING

Take The High Road tells the everyday story
of a West Highland village in the 1980's.
Glendarroch Estate, and the village that
shares its name are situated in the West
of Scotland, a fair bit north of Glasgow.
It's a tight-knit community, the folk at
the "big house" being very much in touch
with what goes on down in the village and
up on the high ground where the crofters
lead a hard life by today's standards.
Many of the traditional ways survive —
but Glendarroch and its people are not
cut off from the problems and pressures
of the modern world.
Now for the first time in paperback — the
story that has endeared itself to viewers
throughout the UK — the story of
Glendarroch from STV's popular serial
Take The High Road.

DON HOUGHTON

TAKE THE HIGH ROAD

DANGER IN THE GLEN

STV's popular serial *Take the High Road* is now an established success, not only in Scotland where it frequently tops the ratings, but also with its enthusiastic daytime viewers throughout the rest of the UK.

Take The High Road is the everyday story of the people who live in the Highland village of Glendarroch, and who work in and around the Estate, from which it takes its name. Mrs Cunningham, "the Lady Laird"; Isabel Blair, the friendly village shopkeeper; and Dougal Lachlan, the droll crofter who's nobody's fool — *all* have become household favourites.

In this second *Take The High Road* book, the reader will enjoy meeting old friends again, and will be intrigued by this tale of a new threat to the Glendarroch Estate.

MICHAEL ELDER